THE OUTRAGEOUS LADY CAROLINE

THE OUTRAGEOUS
LADY CAROLINE

Rachelle Edwards

Chivers Press • Thorndike Press
Bath, England   Waterville, Maine USA

This Large Print edition is published by Chivers Press, England, and by Thorndike Press, USA.

Published in 2003 in the U.K. by arrangement with Robert Hale Ltd.

Published in 2003 in the U.S. by arrangement with Robert Hale Limited.

U.K. Hardcover ISBN 0–7540–8807–3 (Chivers Large Print)
U.K. Softcover   ISBN 0–7540–8808–1 (Camden Large Print)
U.S. Softcover   ISBN 0–7862–4770–3 (General Series Edition)

The text of this Large Print edition is unabridged.
Other aspects of the book may vary from the original edition.

Set in 16 pt. New Times Roman.

Printed in Great Britain on acid-free paper.

British Library Cataloguing in Publication Data available

Library of Congress Cataloging-in-Publication Data

Edwards, Rachelle.
    The outrageous Lady Caroline / Rachelle Edwards.
       p.   cm.
    ISBN 0–7862–4770–3 (lg. print : sc : alk. paper)
    1. England—Fiction. 2. Widows—Fiction. 3. Large type books.
I. Title.
PR6055.D948 O98 2003
823'.914—dc21   2002028729

PROLOGUE

Kilgarron Manor had been built in the reign of Henry the Eighth on the foundations of a much older house. Generations of Kilgarrons had lived there, proud of their ancient line. Altered and added onto through the centuries, it was now the victim of sad neglect.

As she wandered through the formal gardens, Lady Kilgarron viewed the house objectively. It was still a beautiful building, she decided, although she personally felt no emotional attachment to it. Virginia Creeper encroached on the facade, almost obscuring some of the mullions, and a number of slates were missing from the roof. Mentally she noted that the creeper would soon have to be cut back if it were not to obscure the light completely. She would instruct the gardeners to do it, and yet when orders were to be given to servants invariably she shrank from the task. The gardeners were few for such a large estate, but they did not, at least, resent her orders and in the brief year she had been mistress of the Manor she had effected certain improvements to the gardens, long neglected on her arrival. Indoors, however, the house remained unchanged.

There, broken furniture had been consigned to the attics instead of being repaired.

Woodworm burrowed deep into the ancient timbers and valuable tapestries grew more threadbare with each passing year.

Caroline Kilgarron sighed when she thought of all which needed to be done to return the Manor to its former glory. Once she had vowed to do it, but that was what seemed to be a long time ago and she now knew it was beyond her capabilities, not that she harboured any regrets on that score any longer.

Caroline hesitated as she reached the gravelled driveway. A cold wind was blowing across the fields, cutting through the fine shawl which covered her shoulders. She wanted to go indoors now, but the house, she felt, offered no welcome and she hesitated to go in, something she had often done in the past. Now, she told herself sternly, she had no cause to hesitate and she walked quickly up the steps.

Clad in unrelieved black she presented a slight figure, frail almost, and much younger than her twenty years. Being hastily commissioned, the gown was a more fashionable one than any of the others she possessed and she was aware, with more than a small stirring of pleasure, that it became her well.

A footman opened the door and gave her a faint smile. Caroline looked away quickly, for she was certain the smile was an insolent, knowing one. She knew she would be glad to turn her back on the inevitable smirks which followed her wherever she went.

Aware that the servant watched her as she walked up the stairs, her silk skirts rustling against the balusters, Caroline kept her head erect and did not look back. She walked slowly down the long gallery until she reached the drawing room with its fine view of the estate. Caroline did not give it a look; she seated herself at the tambour frame and began to embroider, giving her entire concentration to the emerging pattern on the tapestry.

It was a short time later that a knock on the door caused her to look up and then her startled expression softened into a smile as a young girl came slowly into the room.

'Caro, I've been looking for you everywhere. This house is so big,' she added with a giggle, 'I could lose you for a week.'

Caroline gazed fondly at her sister, younger by three years. 'Up until a few minutes ago I was walking in the gardens.'

'But it's so cold . . .'

'I needed to do some thinking.'

Polly looked at her sister pityingly. 'Dearest, you should not be so rash. The weather is still so inclement; you might have caught a chill. I am certain your slippers are damp.'

Caroline smiled again. 'You must not be so concerned for me, dear. I am perfectly all right, you know.'

Polly remained unconvinced, but then she sat down on a sofa. 'I do worry about you. Of course I do. A widow—and in such shocking circumstances—only a year after you were wed. ' 'Tis enough to make you lose your reason.'

Caroline's needle faltered and then she thrust it into the canvas in a decisive gesture. 'No good can come of dwelling on the past, Polly, my dear. We must look to the future.'

'Oh, you must be the bravest creature alive! I do not think I could have borne it as well as you.' She hesitated before saying, 'I overheard some of the servants saying that Charles Brandon has left. Is it true, Caroline?'

Lady Kilgarron's lips narrowed into a thin line. 'Yes, yes it is true. I allowed him to take the best carriage and team, and he left early this morning.'

'How good of you,' Polly said with admiration shining out of her eyes.

Her sister looked away quickly. 'Now Edgar is dead there is nothing here for Mr Brandon and it was the least I could do.'

'Does he go to London? Oh, if he does he is the most fortunate of men.'

'I believe he intends to travel to the continent—France and Italy. That is what he intimated to me. In any event I do not believe we shall see him again.'

Polly stared down at her hands which were clenched in her lap. 'I cannot own to being

4

sorry. I could not like Mr Brandon, for all he was Sir Edgar's cousin.'

'Mr Brandon did not endear himself to everyone,' Caroline replied in an expressionless voice, adjusting the fischu at her breast. 'You may dismiss him from your mind.'

Polly appeared to have done so for then she said, anxiously again, 'You said you wished to think, dearest. Was it about our future, perchance?'

Caroline gave her sister a quick glance before answering, 'Yes, I have been thinking most carefully for a while and I have decided to sell the Manor.'

There was a momentary silence before Polly leaned forward, stammering, 'Sell Kilgarron Manor? Can you? I mean . . .'

Caroline looked at her sister again and there was no telling expression on her face. 'Of course I can. Why should I not? I have inherited everything from my husband.'

'To whom would you sell, though? Who would want to buy it?'

'There I have had some good fortune. Sir Arthur Taplow approached me after Edgar's funeral. He indicated he was very interested in the Manor if I should consider selling.'

Polly made a noise of exasperation. 'That awful man! I wonder you even speak to him after all the dreadful questions he asked after poor Sir Edgar died.'

Caroline smiled without mirth. 'My dear

5

Polly, Sir Arthur is the local magistrate and it was incumbent upon him to ascertain the exact cause of my husband's death. It *was* an accident and Sir Arthur was obliged to discover the facts of it. He certainly meant no disrespect to *me*.'

Polly sniffed derisively, looking none too convinced, and Caroline went on, 'In any event I have decided to take up his offer, which I believe to be a fair one in view of the extensive repairs which need to be done.'

'Well, I cannot own to feeling at home here,' Polly admitted doubtfully, 'but where shall we go? To one of the cottages on the estate, perchance?'

Caroline got to her feet and walked to the carved oak mantel over which hung the forbidding portrait of one of the Kilgarron ancestors.

'To London.'

'London,' Polly echoed.

'Yes. The matter of your future has been troubling my mind of late.' She walked back across the room, sat down at her sister's side and took hold of her hands. 'Polly, I have made up my mind; *you* are going to have a London Season.'

The girl stared at her uncomprehendingly. 'Caro, have you taken leave of your senses? How can I have a Season?'

For the first time Caroline's eyes lit up with mischief. 'As Sir Edgar Kilgarron's widow who better can introduce you into Society?'

At this Polly Winton laughed. 'Oh, dearest Caro, your attic is most certainly to let! The *ton*. 'Tis impossible and you know it, even if you are Lady Kilgarron. I have no aristocratic connections.'

'You are connected to me which, I assure you, will be sufficient. Polly, dearest, you *will* have the opportunity of making a brilliant marriage.'

Polly stared at her sister in astonishment. 'You truly believe it possible, do you not?'

'Oh yes,' Caroline breathed.

'Would I not need a portion?'

'You shall have one. Money is no problem. It will come from my late husband's estate. We are going to take a house in the fashionable part of Town, ride in the Park, go everywhere fashionable Society goes. Do you not want that, Polly?'

The girl's eyes shone at the prospect. 'Oh, yes indeed, but I would be too afraid, Caro.'

'Nonsense. You will contrive very well. It will be a new start for us both.'

'But I have no notion how to behave in elevated Society.'

'You will learn, my dear; we both shall learn. You do wish to wed, do you not?'

'Oh yes,' the girl breathed.

'There is no one hereabouts suitable, certainly not the stableboy.' The girl blushed and her sister went on, 'Oh, I am well aware of the friendship between you and Harris.'

'There is nothing wrong with that, Caro. He is the only one with whom I feel at ease.'

Caroline gave her a sympathetic look. 'I do understand how you feel, dearest, believe me I do. I felt similarly lost when I married Edgar and came to live in the Manor. I don't advocate you should marry Royalty or even a duke, but I have the means to secure you a good match by means of my own marriage. Do you truly not wish to take advantage of that?'

'You are so good, dear Caro, and I do wish to see London and enjoy all the diversions of which I have heard. You have schooled me well during this past year and as a result I feel more of this Society than any other.'

'Then there is no further need to discuss the matter. We shall go as soon as everything is settled here.'

'You make me believe it is possible so perhaps you will also make a brilliant match, Caro. You are too young to remain a widow. It pains me to witness your situation.'

Caroline's eyes clouded. 'You must not trouble your head on that score. I am determined never to marry again.' At the sight of her sister's troubled expression Caroline smiled. 'If I can see *you* well settled I shall be more than satisfied.'

'I shall be so afraid; all those grand people, used to the ways of Society. I shall be so shabby too. Oh, Caro, I cannot . . .'

'Fudge! By the time the new Season begins we shall both have new gowns suitable for every occasion, and from what I have perceived newcomers are eagerly sought out and afforded every hospitality.'

'The prospect is exciting and yet frightening too. What are you to do about everything here? The servants. Do you intend to dismiss them all? It would be too cruel.'

Caroline drew back. 'Naturally they will become Sir Arthur's responsibility. I am sure they will all continue in his employ.'

'Do you not intend to take even your own maid?'

Caroline looked down at her clasped hands. 'Foskitt was appointed by Mrs Cox on Sir Edgar's orders. The time has come, I think, for me to choose my own. Besides, when we remove to London I shall need a maid accustomed to fashionable styles. I intend for us to be all the crack, you know!'

Polly gazed at her sister for a moment or two. 'Caroline, you have changed greatly in this last year.'

Lady Kilgarron got to her feet, smiling tightly. 'Oh yes, my dear, that is most certainly true. No one is more aware of that than I.'

Her smile grew broader as she turned to her sister once again, 'And now, my dear, I am going to ring for a servant and we shall enjoy a dish of tea together whilst we discuss our plans!'

CHAPTER ONE

The Drury Lane Theatre was packed from pit to gallery with a fashionable array of people, all eager to see the famed Sarah Siddons in one of her best known roles—Ophelia.

Every box was filled with important personages, arrayed in fine silks and jewels—men and women alike. In one of the boxes, surrounded by her companions, one of the foremost hostesses of the *ton*, the Countess of Farrowdale, quizzed the auditorium thoroughly, pausing now and again to cast an acid remark to her companions on the contents of the boxes.

'I see that old Cannonville is still in pursuit of Daisy Mountford. When will the old fool realise it is marriage *she* pursues? After three husbands it is obvious she is addicted!'

The others laughed and a foppish gentleman, named Lord Carlingdale said, 'Have you seen Sally Bleasedale's hairdo, Lady Farrowdale?'

'La! I believe everyone as far as Kensington can see it, even from here. It lacks only a step-ladder to reach the top!'

The party laughed again as she added, 'Horatia Pendlebury is here with Johnny Fortescue. I do believe she has a different lover for every day of the week.' Just then her gaze came to rest on Caroline Kilgarron's box and she gasped. 'Who is that?' she cried and all eyes centred on that box.

'Oh indeed. You must mean the ravishingly beautiful creature in black,' replied one of her companions, a painted and patched dandy who could not sit down because of the tightness of his breeches. He had to content himself to lean against a gilded pillar for the duration.

'I have no notion,' another replied, 'but I would be obliged to anyone who could do me the service of telling me.'

'I cannot conceive why we do not know her,' Lady Farrowdale continued, still staring at Caroline through her quizzing glass. 'She is obviously a person of consequence.'

'Just look at those diamonds,' another gasped. 'Has anyone ever seen such fine jewels?'

Lady Farrowdale tapped the incredulous woman on the hand with her fan. 'My own are much finer.'

The woman blushed. 'Quite so, Lady Farrowdale. I did not mean . . .'

The countess was tapping her teeth thoughtfully with her fan. 'I own I am intrigued by this person. It is inconceivable that there is someone I do not know.'

Her companions did not know whether to laugh or not and one or two did venture to do so, albeit halfheartedly.

'I must make sure of her identity,' the

countess declared.

'Ha! Too late! I have already done so,' Lord Farrowdale announced as he came into the box.

The other members of the party looked to him in astonishment as he took a pinch of snuff quite unconcernedly, spilling a good deal of it in the process.

'I could well have guessed,' his wife admitted in a resigned tone of voice, 'that where a fetching chit is concerned my husband would know everything. Tell us, Farrowdale, have you also determined the plan of her bedchamber yet?'

The others laughed yet again at the countess's wit and her husband replied, not a mite dismayed, 'Not yet, my dear, but no doubt I will do so before the night is over.'

'Do not keep us in suspense,' urged another lady, whose towering hairdo wobbled precariously every time she moved her head. 'Who is the divine creature? We are all consumed with curiosity, are we not?'

The others murmured their agreement. Lord Farrowdale stared across to Caroline's box and when it seemed she met his gaze he bowed deeply, but she made no sign that she had noticed him.

'I shall tell you on the understanding that I have first claim on her. Gentlemen, is it agreed? The filly is mine.'

'Oh really, Farrowdale,' his wife

complained, 'by the morrow every buck in Town will be beating a path to her door. What time will she have for a bosky old lecher like you?'

The others laughed too and Lord Farrowdale brought out a lace-edged handkerchief which he pressed to his lips. 'Not everyone shares your scathing opinion of me, Augusta.'

'Fudge! I look upon you kindly, which is precisely my point.'

'If that is your opinion I shall keep my knowledge to myself and be damned to all of you!'

The others began to murmur and one or two cajoled him gently.

'Oh, come now, Farrowdale, own that you are longing to tell us.'

'I'll wager she is a merchant's daughter out to catch a title,' Lord Carlingdale suggested.

'No, no,' another argued. 'Her gown is exquisite so she must be a French seamstress seeking patronage.'

'With those jewels,' scoffed Lady Farrowdale.

'You are all quite wrong,' Lord Farrowdale told them in a laconic voice, enjoying himself now.

'The creature is quite plainly a doxy displaying her charms.'

Still Lord Farrowdale continued to smile.

'Who is the mouse-like creature with her?'

'A companion, I dare say.'

'She is too well dressed for that, I fancy. Besides, they are both so very young.'

Lady Farrowdale snapped shut her fan. 'By the morrow we shall all know, so ' 'tis useless to tease our brains in this way. Desmond, you look pale. Are you unwell?'

Lord Farrowdale was startled at the change of topic. 'No, my dear, just this new powder which I bought only yesterday on the advice it would flatter me.'

'Nothing short of a miracle would do that,' his wife replied.

Looking a mite discomforted he answered, 'Oh, very well, I shall purchase a pot of my usual type first thing on the morrow.'

'If you are not pursuing our mystery lady at that time,' whispered one of his friends who winked conspiratorially.

'Do you intend to tell us or do you not?' his wife asked pointedly.

'Oh very well, my dear. I was only gammoning you all. The lady,' he said, clearing his throat noisily, 'is the widow of a Sir Edgar Kilgarron who died earlier this year. There is nothing mysterious about her, you see.'

'So young to be a widow! ' a lady exclaimed.

Lord Farrowdale cast her an irritated look. 'My dear Virginia, pray allow me to continue.'

'I do beg your pardon,' the woman replied with a giggle. 'Do continue, Lord Farrowdale. We are all exceedingly anxious to hear what you have to say.'

The others laughed and he went on, 'She has taken a house in Queen Square for the Season in order to launch her sister into Society.'

'So that is the other chit. 'Tis to be hoped she possesses a sizeable fortune, for her face will never be that.'

Lady Farrowdale glanced at her husband. 'Your tenacity is as ever overwhelming. How did you come by this remarkable information?'

The earl sank down into his seat, bringing out a fan which he began to swish to and fro.

' 'Twas easy, my love. For the consideration of half a guinea the lackey on duty outside the box revealed all.'

'No doubt Farrowdale is not the only one importuning him,' commented Lord Carlingdale, 'and I'm sure the fellow will be set up for life by the end of the evening!'

'Does anyone know Sir Edgar Kilgarron?' someone asked, and the others looked blank.

'No doubt he was a member of the rustic gentry,' Lady Farrowdale mused, 'but even so, if it is true she is his widow, I shall be obliged to call on her very soon.'

'Oh, indeed you must, my love,' her husband agreed, 'and so must we all. It would only be correct.'

His wife smiled behind her fan. 'I am convinced we may rely upon you to pay your respects.'

'I like to maintain the proprieties.'

'That is something you do not do,' his wife rejoined. 'However, we shall not be alone. 'Tis obvious the entire audience here is buzzing with speculation about her. I doubt if poor Mrs Siddons will make any impression whatsoever tonight. Ah, I believe it is about to begin. Even now I can declare this to be a most diverting evening.'

*   *   *

Polly gazed around the theatre, her eyes alight with excitement.

'Caro, this is the most exciting evening of my life!'

Her sister cast her an indulgent look. 'I must own that it is, my dear, but it is not done to show it. At all times we must exhibit nothing but utter boredom, or at the very least indifference.'

'That is impossible. I cannot conceive how you are keeping calm. It is enough that we are here and about to see Mrs Siddons act, but you must certainly have noticed how everyone is quizzing us. We are attracting more attention than the actors—more like you, though, rather than me.'

'I should have been bitterly disappointed if we didn't,' Caroline observed, 'and you are wrong in assuming it is only me they are quizzing. There is a young man in the next box who cannot stop looking at you.'

Polly ventured to give him a quick glance, smiling shyly. 'I never dreamed anything could be so exciting.'

'We have only just begun, you must recall. This is our first social event. If everything goes to plan many more will follow. You must have every opportunity to meet young men of wealth and breeding.'

Polly giggled behind her fan. 'Oh, Caro, I shall not know what to say to any of them.'

'I am convinced you will contrive when the time comes. You need only smile and look pretty. Nothing more will be required, I assure you.'

'I hope you may be right about that,' her sister answered doubtfully. Then brightening said, 'I often dream about the man I will marry, but I really cannot imagine him at all.'

Caroline looked at her indulgently again, putting a gentle hand over hers. 'I pray your dreams will always be so happy.'

'How can they not be? Everything is even better than I envisaged.'

Caroline looked suddenly thoughtful. 'I really think we should have taken a house in Mayfair rather than where we are.'

'Mayfair might well be all the crack now, but our house in Queen Square is such a fine one, as fine as any I have ever seen.'

'You will see much better before long, my dear.'

'Even so I did not think . . .'

'Did you think we should share a loft above a stable, Polly?' Caroline asked gently.

Her sister blushed. 'No, of course I didn't, but . . .' Just then she noticed Lady Farrowdale. 'Oh, who is that lady in the enormous wig who is quizzing us all the time? She is quite imposing. I am sure she must be of great importance.'

'I have no notion who she can be, but I don't doubt we shall find out before long.'

'Your diamonds are so magnificent; they are certain to excite interest. Oh, you do look so fine, Caro. I could not hope to emulate you, even though you have spent a fortune on my gowns. You were always so handsome even before you wed Sir Edgar, and now you have a new maid who is *au fait* with all the fashions, you look as fine as anyone here.'

'You exaggerate, dearest. Some of the most beautiful women in London are here tonight, but I must own that Beth is a treasure. I was very fortunate to have found her.'

'She is much more pleasant than Foskitt too. *She* was always so intimidating, disapproving too I thought, although I could never have ventured to say so whilst we were at the Manor.'

Caroline sighed. 'Everything which happened at Kilgarron Manor is past and gone, Polly, including Foskitt, and it need never affect us again.'

The performance was about to begin, although few enough conversations ceased and young men continued to catcall from the pit throughout the evening. Caroline's box continued to be the prime source of interest to all those who had paid dearly to see Sarah Siddons.

*   *   *

Lifelong habits were hard to give up, and the morning after their visit to Drury Lane Caroline and Polly were up early. After breakfast they took a ride down Oxford Street before visiting the excellent shops for which the street was becoming known. Although they had purchased almost everything they required before the Season began, the marvellous shops of which London boasted attracted them endlessly, and scarce a day went by without a visit to one emporium or another. Lady Kilgarron became so well-known, proprietors rushed personally to hand her down from her carriage and show her their latest wares.

'I cannot help but feel guilty at the amount of poor Sir Edgar's money we have spent since our arrival in London,' Polly complained.

Her sister, resting against the squabs of their smart new carriage smiled. 'Sir Edgar, when he was alive, was a free-spending man, so I am persuaded he would understand it in us.'

They arrived back in Queen Square to be informed by the head footman that several personages had called in their absence. As Caroline removed the hat she had worn at an angle on top of her dark, powdered curls, Polly examined the calling cards which had been left in their absence.

'Caro, only look!' she cried after a moment. 'Such people of consequence! Sir Francis Tushberry, Lady Crickleston, Lord Do . . . oh, Lady Stannard. Caro, there's an *invitation* here to a rout at the house of the Earl and Countess of Farrowdale in Manchester Square!'

Caroline remained calm in the face of her sister's growing excitement. 'Dearest, it is no more than I would expect after our debut last night. We created a great deal of interest and speculation so there will be many more callers and invitations before long, I fancy.'

'I cannot understand your being so calm about it. One would almost think you planned it this way.'

'In a sense I did. I knew that presenting myself would be to no avail; our peers, Polly, must come to us.'

'What a scheming minx you are, Caro. Such cleverness, and then, to think, we were actually *out* when they called!'

'I am quite persuaded none of them would have expected us to be in. They will come back you may be sure.'

Polly shook her head, her eyes agleam.

20

'There are times when you are like a stranger to me, Caroline.'

Lady Kilgarron put her hand out to her sister. 'Come, let us go into the drawing room and examine those cards at leisure. The fact that we were not at home can only inflame interest in us further.'

'You do intend to accept the invitations,' Polly asked worriedly. 'It is not in your plans to refuse?'

Caroline laughed and her sister suddenly realised it was something she rarely did of late.

'Yes, we shall most certainly accept them all. That, after all, is the object, but it does no harm to create a little mystery whilst we are about it.'

'You are a veritable schemer, Caro,' Polly said in amazement. 'I believe you have it in you to become a duchess if you set your mind upon it.'

Caroline laughed again. 'I shall be glad enough to see you reach that position.'

'You cannot be serious!'

Caroline gave her a long, considering look before answering, 'Oh yes, yes I am.'

Polly blushed and they began to examine in more detail the cards which had been left. Then, after some time, they were interrupted by a footman bearing the gilt-edged calling card of the Earl of Farrowdale.

Caroline took the card from the salver, considering it for a moment before tapping it against her wrist. 'I wonder which fop this one can be?'

'Perchance he is not a fop; he may be the young man who sat in the box next to ours.'

Caroline gave her sister a sharp look as the footman said, 'His lordship earnestly begs a few moments of your time, my lady.'

Caroline looked amused then, her sister afraid, before she got to her feet. 'By all means show him in, Tompkins, so we may satisfy our curiosity.'

'What shall we find to say to him?' Polly asked when the servant had gone. 'I am certain I shall say something stupid.'

'Let Lord Farrowdale speak to us first,' her sister replied. 'We can then speak in answer to him.'

Caroline was hard-pressed to hide a smile as the aging dandy was ushered into the drawing room. Wearing a coat of rich brocade, he had heavy powder on his face too, and several black patches.

He bowed low before the two women. 'Lady Kilgarron, I am honoured indeed to present my compliments to you personally.'

Both Caroline and Polly sank into deep curtseys. 'We are honoured too, my lord,' Caroline said as she straightened up. 'Allow me to present my sister, Miss Polly Winton.'

Lord Farrowdale transferred his attention, rather reluctantly, to the young girl, saying absently, 'Charming, utterly charming.' Then he feasted his eyes on Caroline once more. 'And you, my dear. Last night I feared would prove to be a mere figment of my imagination, but you are even lovelier in the light of day.'

Caroline lowered her eyes demurely. 'Lord Farrowdale, I am overcome by your flattery.'

' 'Tis no such thing, my dear. The plain truth, no more and even so no words could do justice to you.'

In response Caroline dimpled prettily. 'Won't you sit with us a while, my lord?'

Eagerly the earl seated himself, but to his obvious disappointment Caroline sat down in a chair a few feet away when he would have clearly preferred her to join him on the sofa.

'We were delighted to receive the invitation to your lordship's rout on Tuesday next. We were just discussing it before you arrived.'

'Lady Farrowdale and I hope you and . . . er . . . Miss Winton,' glancing at Polly who sat wide-eyed watching him, 'will be able to attend at such short notice.'

'You must know, Lord Farrowdale, my sister and I are only recently come to London, and as yet our engagement book is not overfull.'

The earl paused to take a pinch of snuff, brushing the spillage from his breeches. 'An instance soon to be mended, my dear,' he answered, wiping his face with a lace-edged handkerchief. 'Your presence will be required at any assembly which aspires to be brilliant.'

Caroline inclined her head. 'You really are

too kind.'

He glanced at Polly as if hoping she would leave and then when she remained seated he looked at Caroline again. 'You are sadly widowed, I believe . . .'

'Alas, that is true.'

He eyed her speculatively for a moment before saying, ' 'Tis sad, I own, but you are young and there will be much pleasure for you in the future.'

'My hopes for the future rest with Miss Winton.'

'Quite so. A most admirable sentiment.'

Caroline got to her feet. 'Lord Farrowdale, I have enjoyed our conversation very much but it is very regrettable that I must end it now. My sister and I have an engagement.'

Polly looked slightly bewildered and the earl got to his feet, wheezing slightly.

'It was good of you to receive me.'

'It has been a great pleasure and one I hope we may repeat before too long.'

Lord Farrowdale bowed low over her hand. 'You may be certain we shall, my dear.'

He gave Polly a last nod before leaving. The moment he had gone Polly turned to her sister.

'Caro, how could you dismiss him so calmly? Lord Farrowdale! I could not believe the evidence of my own ears.'

'It would be a mistake to be too available. Besides, I had endured enough of his lecherous looks.'

Polly giggled. 'He was rather obvious about it, wasn't he? But I fear that many men will look at you thus, Caro.'

'I am well able to counter it in Lord Farrowdale, and in others too.'

'I can scarce wait until Tuesday for the rout, but shall we be able to dance well enough for a fashionable rout?'

'Monsieur Grillet was most satisfied with our dancing ability. He taught us well, so you must not be faint-hearted.

'Come, Polly, put on your new blue bonnet and we shall ride in the Park today for the benefit of all those who did not see us at Drury Lane last night.'

At this suggestion the girl squealed with delight and rushed towards the door, laughing.

'Whatever the end result might be, I am already quite certain that this Season is going to be the greatest fun!'

CHAPTER TWO

The public rooms of Lord and Lady Farrowdale's home was one seething mass of people. Without exception all those present were dressed in the height of fashion, jewellery glittered everywhere on both men and women. An orchestra played in the main salon for those who wished to dance and card tables had been set up in two or three of the smaller rooms for the many who enjoyed gambling.

On her arrival with Polly, Caroline found they were very much the object of interest. Apart from the initial and obligatory greeting, Lady Farrowdale contrived to ignore the newcomers, something noted by Caroline but because it was a veritable squeeze few others would have done so.

The sisters possessed a great array of gowns suited to all occasions and the night of the Farrowdale's rout warranted the wearing of their finest. Caroline had discarded her mourning as more than six months had elapsed since Sir Edgar's death and she wore a green silk lustring gown of the latest Paris mode. Diamonds glittered in the light of a thousand wax candles, at her throat, wrists and in the elaborate coiffeur created by her new maid.

Polly, on the other hand, as befitted an

unmarried girl, was attired in a more modest manner, in cream brocade, her sister's pearls around her throat. Both young ladies were generally held to be quite handsome by the many influential critics present, although the younger appeared plain by comparison to her sister.

His wife's example was certainly not copied by Lord Farrowdale. As soon as he was able he attached himself to Caroline's side and only a few determined gentlemen contrived to engage her for some of the sets. Whilst Caroline had no real liking for the earl, whom she recognised as a practised rake, she was glad enough of his flattering attention and the way he introduced her to many guests of great importance.

If she was asked many questions she would rather not have answered, Caroline was quite willing to contrive as best she could, for Polly was wandering around with bright eyes and flushed cheeks and, more importantly, she scarcely lacked a partner for the dancing. It was a very satisfactory state of affairs.

'I cannot understand why you have not come up to Town before,' Lord Farrowdale said as they joined the set being made up for a country dance.

She smiled at him sweetly, aware that they were the object of interest to all around them.

'Kilgarron preferred the country life, Lord Farrowdale, and I am myself country bred.'

' 'Tis no wonder Sir Edgar was of such a mind with the charms of his wife to keep him at home, and in view of the score of admirers you have already acquired he was sensible to keep you there too, but I do trust you are enjoying your stay and have no plans to return to Kilgarron Manor.'

After a moment's pause she answered, 'Kilgarron Manor holds so many sad memories, my lord, I am in no hurry to return.'

To her great surprise his eyes sparkled with tears. 'My poor, poor dear,' he murmured.

Quickly Caroline went on, 'We intend to stay for at least the duration of this Season. Beyond that we have no plans.'

'It is likely you will receive countless invitations to house parties for the summer months.'

Such a possibility had not yet occurred to Caroline, but it pleased her to think it might be so.

'Both Miss Winton and myself are overwhelmed at the hospitality and interest displayed by everyone we have met. Our appointment book is full now for the next three months.'

'I am delighted to hear you say so, Lady Kilgarron. That means without doubt we shall often be in each other's company.'

Caroline noted, not for the first time, that her sister was being partnered by the same young man they had seen at Drury Lane. He had a pleasing appearance, if rather unexceptional, and Caroline was glad to note that he was not too dandified although modishly dressed.

Noticing her interest Lord Farrowdale said slyly, 'It is evident that the evening is a great success as far as Miss Winton is concerned.'

Immediately Caroline returned her attention to the earl. 'I have noted her prediliction for that particular young man, but I confess I am not acquainted with him. Do you happen to know who he is, Lord Farrowdale?'

Obviously irritated at having his attention diverted from Caroline, he replied, 'He is connected to the Devonshires. Do you go to Lord Caranmere's on the morrow, my dear?'

Caroline's step almost faltered. 'The Devonshires!' she gasped. 'Are you certain?'

He laughed. 'I have been acquainted with Mr Underwood since he was a very small boy in leading strings. You must understand, my dear, that Thomas Underwood is related on the distaff side of the family and as such is of modest means. He is a younger son, you see, and the Minister of the Meynsham living.'

The country dance had come to an end. Caroline looked at him in dismay and her partner threw back his head and laughed loudly before saying, 'There is time, beautiful one, for Miss Winton to make her final choice from more eligible suitors.'

'Oh, I did not mean . . .' she began to protest.

'Your ambition is quite understandable, my dear. However, many a young buck will undoubtedly pursue Miss Winton in the hope of winning you.'

That was something which was becoming more evident, much to Caroline's vexation. 'It will be a fruitless effort, Lord Farrowdale. I am not in the least interested in callow young men.'

His eyes were alight with speculation. 'It warms my heart to hear you say so.'

Acutely discomforted she added, 'Moreover, I have no intention of ever marrying again.'

He laughed once more and took a pinch of snuff. 'I am persuaded that may be an added bounty for their efforts.'

Reminded about the morals prevalent in Society, once again Caroline felt discomforted until a moment later when she became aware of a young man who was leaning against a wall. Immediately she was diverted from her discomforting thoughts. His arms were folded in front of him and he was watching her from beneath lowered lids. His entire demeanour spoke of utter boredom, not the fashionably feigned kind, but true boredom. Used now to undisguised admiration in the expressions of all who looked upon her, Caroline smiled uncertainly, but that elicited no response which served to puzzle, and to intrigue, her further.

What had first caught her attention was the fact that he was dressed unlike most of the other men present. Taller than many, he wore no wig, rather his own dark hair tied back with a black silk ribbon. There were neither paint nor patches on his face, and his clothes were of a much plainer kind than anyone else sported. His coat was of some plain dark cloth and his waistcoat was adorned by only one gold chain.

'Will you allow me the pleasure of escorting you into supper, Lady Kilgarron?' Lord Farrowdale asked and Caroline reluctantly returned her attention to her host.

'I would be honoured, my lord, but I cannot allow you to neglect your other guests on my account.'

'As you can plainly see, they are far from neglected and I can escort but one of them into supper. If it be the most beautiful lady in the room, then it is my good fortune.'

His interest in her, flattering at first, was fast becoming embarrassing, but reminding herself that she had come to London only for Polly's sake, she gave him a smile of aquiescence. Their progress to the supper room was followed with great interest, especially by a frosty-faced Lady Farrowdale.

*　　　*　　　*

Caroline tossed to and fro in the four-poster bed which dwarfed her, tormented by dreams which had once occurred distressingly often. Now they visited her with less frequency, but Caroline dreaded them all the same.

She and Polly had returned home late from the Farrowdale's rout the previous evening, Polly full of excitement, chattering endlessly about every aspect of the rout. Whilst Caroline was glad they had been such a success she was also a little troubled by Lord Farrowdale's obsessive pursuit of her. She was aware, however, that the patronage of such people was very necessary if Polly was to contract a suitable marriage and the attention of those such as Lord Farrowdale would have to be endured until that was achieved.

Beth, Caroline's new maid, was on hand to undress her mistress and, unused to London hours, Caroline soon afterwards fell exhausted into her bed, but sleep was not the panacea for which she had hoped.

Suddenly she sat up in the bed, shivering slightly, her eyes wide with fear. After a moment she realised that the dream had ended and she sank back into the pillows with a sigh of relief. Her hand shook slightly as she reached for the tinder box and lit the candle which stood on a table at the side of the bed. Welcome light flooded the room.

Foolish to let such dreams torment her, she thought. And then as she realised morning was not yet upon them, she also noticed that the curtains were not closed, something she had seen Beth do before she had retired. Moreover, they were moving slightly in a breeze which caused the candle flame to flicker.

At almost the precise moment Caroline got out of bed and reached for a shawl which she wrapped around her, a sudden wind rattled the casement open. Panic struck at her, for she knew the windows were never left open at night. It was well known that the night air was positively harmful to a sleeper.

At Kilgarron Manor Caroline had never thought about the safety of her jewels, for they had always remained in her late husband's safe-keeping except for the rare occasions when he required her to wear them. But this was London, home of every kind of crime, and Caroline feared that she was about to become the victim of a robber.

She had not even managed to push her feet into her slippers before the curtain moved again, causing her to draw back in alarm. A shadowy figure emerged from behind the half open curtain, causing Caroline to stiffen with fear. She clasped the shawl about her breast as her eyes opened wide with surprise, recognising the intruder even though the room was filled with shadows.

'Lord Farrowdale!'

'Hush, my dear. We do not want to waken

the entire household, do we?'

His wig was askew, his face florid, and it was evident he was much the worse for drink. Caroline's fear turned to anger.

'That is precisely what I intend to do very soon, Lord Farrowdale. Why are you here in this manner?'

He came further into the room, laughing softly. 'Surely that is evident, my dear. Oh, I am impressed by your modesty. Your anger is delightful too, but you need have no fear of your reputation, fair Caroline, if that is what disturbs you. I shall be gone even before your servants are abroad.'

'You shall be gone immediately,' she retorted, her breast heaving with indignation.

Still he was unabashed. 'Oh, I cannot help but feel you are gammoning me, my dear. The moment I clapped eyes upon you, I knew you were made for my love. Admit that you feel it too.'

When Caroline did nothing more than step back in alarm he said, 'See, I have something for you to gladden your heart. You will find me a most generous lover.'

Caroline gasped at his audacity, for at the end of his finger dangled a diamond and emerald bracelet of unusual design which sparkled in the candlelight. Startled, Caroline could only stare at it. She knew it must be worth a small fortune and his devotion momentarily touched her until she cast her mind back to the previous evening and then her anger mounted again.

'Lord Farrowdale, is that not the bracelet you won at Faro from Lady Bleasedale last night?'

'It is indeed and a magnificent specimen, I assure you.'

'You cannot believe I would actually accept it from you.'

'It would not be thought amiss, my dear.'

He tossed the bracelet onto the counterpane and would be delayed no longer. Caroline flinched away as he bounded forward, clasping her to his chest. The scent of his chypre perfume, intermingled with the smell of alcohol, filled her head, making her feel nauseous. She struggled against the kisses he feverishly and clumsily pressed to her cheeks and neck, but he was oblivious to all else save his passion.

At last she managed to free herself from his obnoxious embrace, thrusting him across the room with all her might, where he almost upset the washstand.

He gasped at the unexpectedness of her rejection as he struggled to right the washstand. 'Lady Kilgarron, you go too far.'

'Lord Farrowdale, you are a miserable coxcomb,' she answered breathlessly.

He straightened up as she re-adjusted the shawl, but then she flinched once more at the gleam which came into his eye. 'But you are more woman that I have ever encountered,' he said as he lunged forward once more.

Caroline was ready for him this time and she deftly moved to one side, her hand fumbling beneath the pillow. Before the earl could take hold of her again Caroline had brought out the tiniest of pistols, so small it could be held in the palm of her hand.

It trembled slightly in her hand as she pointed it at him. 'Stay where you are!' she ordered, and he halted a few steps away from her, his eyes widening in surprise.

'Madame, what are you about? ' 'Tis I, Desmond Farrowdale.'

'I am fully aware just who you are, my lord, and it would please me if you would leave my bedchamber with no further delay.'

He stared at the pistol with a comical astonishment, but Caroline could not laugh. Lord Farrowdale did not laugh either; he was well aware that however dainty the pistol it was nonetheless deadly, more usually carried in a lady's muff in the event of an attack by footpads or highwaymen.

'Lady Kilgarron!' he gasped, backing away, much to her relief. 'I cannot credit this.'

'I have no wish to be found with a dead nobleman in my bedchamber,' she said in a slightly breathless voice, 'nor do I wish to alarm my sister, so be pleased to go quickly. Now, Lord Farrowdale.'

Foxed, he nevertheless recognised that she

was deadly serious and he began to edge, rather unsteadily, towards the door.

With the pistol still pointed towards him, Caroline said, 'Not that way, my lord. The way you came—through the window.'

He began to bluster but still hurried towards the window, climbing onto the balcony with more haste than dignity. As he gave her one last, bewildered look, she added, 'One more point, Lord Farrowdale; do not seek to boast of a conquest to your cronies, for a like welcome is awaiting anyone of them who dares to emulate you.'

The moment he had gone she rushed to the window and secured it before pulling the curtain across. After that she went back to the bed, sinking down onto it, for her knees were suddenly weak. The pistol hung limply in her hand now and she let out a great sigh before lying back against the pillows. She shivered slightly although the room was not cold and she knew that sleep was most certainly gone for good that night.

CHAPTER THREE

When Beth arrived the following morning to wake her mistress with the customary cup of chocolate she was surprised to find Caroline awake and ready to be dressed.

' 'Tis a fine mornin', ma'am,' she told the uncaring Caroline.

As she drew back the curtains to admit the early morning sun Caroline looked fearfully towards the balcony in the unlikely event the earl was still there. Even though the pistol still remained by her pillow she felt she would never be able to sleep easily again in London.

'Which gown shall I set out?' the maid asked, going towards the press.

'The brown tabby,' Caroline answered automatically.

'Shall I prepare the red powder for your hair, ma'am? It'll match well with the brown silk.'

'No, don't trouble today, Beth. I shall leave my hair unpowdered.'

Beth shot her mistress a curious look as she busied herself preparing the morning toilette. As she did so Caroline quickly wrapped the bracelet which Lord Farrowdale had left and handed it to her maid.

'Have one of the footmen deliver this to Lady Bleasdale, Beth, as soon as possible.' She hesitated before smiling slightly. 'He is to say it is with Lord Farrowdale's compliments. Is that clear?'

It was evident that Beth was puzzled by Caroline's manner, but it was not her place to question anything her mistress did and she nodded. When she had gone Caroline's smile faded slightly, for she was now worried, fearing that Lord Farrowdale would exert his considerable social influence against her. She needed no one to tell her he could ruin their entree into elevated social circles before it had even begun. Fervently she hoped this would not transpire, but even for Polly's sake she could not suffer the earl's lovemaking.

It transpired that Caroline had little time to ponder on the vexing possibilities of the night's events, for she was soon accosted by one of the maids who appeared to be in something of a pucker.

'Lady Kilgarron, Miss Winton begs me to tell you she wishes to be excused any activity today as she feels unwell.'

All thoughts of Lord Farrowdale went from Caroline's mind now as she hurried to her sister's room to find Polly looking pale and uncomfortable in her bed.

'Dearest, what ails you?'

' 'Tis nothing, Caro; only that I feel less robust than usual, possibly because we had such a late night.'

Caroline was not so easily convinced. Her

sister was no sickly society chit, lying on a daybed and enjoying ill health. She pressed her hand to Polly's brow, saying with heartfelt relief, 'There seems to be no fever so we may rest assured on that score, but I have long been aware that the air of London is unhealthy. Contagions of all types flourish here.'

'Caro, I beg you not to get into a pucker. All I need is some more sleep. Truly, dearest.'

Her sister still remained unconvinced. 'If there is no improvement by this afternoon I shall call in a physician to physick you. Only the best man will do, mind you, certainly no quacks or charlatans will be tolerated.'

Polly laughed. 'We have enjoyed nothing but the best since we arrived.'

'I intended no different. Sleep now, dearest. In the meantime I shall prepare a dose of mercury water which should set you to rights.'

'There is nothing to get into a pucker about, Caro. I am persuaded it is merely a reaction to all the excitement of the last few days. I ate far too much last night, although I cannot be sorry for it. The devilled crab was delicious, oh, and the duckling was superb too. Did you ever see such a feast? And then, of course, I was not obliged to sit out one set afterwards.'

'So I noticed,' Caroline answered with a grin.

'You have no call to take that attitude. Everyone made a great fuss of you too.'

'It was most diverting, I must own.'

'Lord Farrowdale is quite taken by you,' Polly went on, and her sister was not glad of the reminder. 'How odd it seems that married ladies and gentlemen pay no heed to their spouses. I am sure I shall demand fidelity once I am wed.'

'No doubt you will be deserving of it, but whilst we are here we shall be obliged to learn to tolerate the ways of the ton if we are to be a part of it.'

'His devotion to you is quite understandable, Caro, but you could not possibly want him as a gallant.'

'Definitely not, and he is not about to become one, you may be sure.'

Polly smiled with satisfaction and her sister moved away from the bed. 'I still hope that an eligible gentleman will cause you to throw your cap over the windmill.'

Caroline paused by the door. 'That is not the object of our stay, Polly.'

'Oh, but you cannot wear the willow for Sir Edgar for ever.'

Caroline's eyes grew bleak but her sister could not have seen it. 'Do not let it trouble your head, my love. Sleep now if you can and I shall go and raid the medicine chest.'

*   *   *

Far from being improved by the afternoon

Polly confessed to feeling much worse after a lengthy sleep, complaining now of both pain and nausea. Caroline viewed her sister with a mixture of anxiety and panic and was wondering which of the fashionable physicians to summon when a footman announced the arrival of the Countess of Farrowdale.

Standing outside her sisters bedchamber, Caroline stared at the card in disbelief, all manner of discomforting thoughts milling around in her head.

'Lady Farrowdale,' she gasped. 'Oh, I cannot receive *her*. Pray tell her ladyship I am not at home.'

However, before the servant had any chance to do her bidding Lady Farrowdale came into the hall. She immediately looked up as she stripped off her gloves and espied Caroline who was on the landing.

'Ah, Lady Kilgarron, how fortunate to have found you at home.'

Full of foreboding Caroline came down the stairs, resigned to facing this rather forbidding matron. After last night, Lady Farrowdale was just about the last person she would have chosen to see.

'Why, Lady Farrowdale, how kind of you to call. You are very welcome,' she lied, managing all the same to inject a little enthusiasm into her voice. 'Will you be pleased to come into my sitting room?'

'Gladly.'

She handed the footman her gloves before accompanying Caroline to her sitting room. She glanced about her briefly, missing nothing, Caroline was sure.

'A charming room,' was the countess's verdict.

Although Caroline was mature beyond her years, mainly because of her early marriage to Sir Edgar, she felt nevertheless intimidated by this forceful and important lady, who seated herself by the fire before smiling at the frightened young woman.

'Your rout, Lady Farrowdale, was magnificent,' Caroline said quickly to break the uncomfortable silence that had suddenly come between them.

The countess had been surveying the younger woman quite as blatantly as she had at Drury Lane. 'I am obliged to hear you say so. One does try, especially as everyone else is so determined to make a more brilliant evening.'

'That, I am persuaded, is quite impossible.'

The countess smiled slightly before glancing around. 'I do hope I have not called at an inopportune moment.' She returned her attention to Caroline. 'You seem rather . . . overset.'

Caroline sat down then. 'Oh no, not at all. At least . . .' Lady Farrowdale's eyebrows rose expressively and Caroline added, 'My sister is a trifle indisposed and I was, when you arrived, contemplating summoning Sir James

Eversleigh.'

'I am sorry to hear that Miss Winton is ill. I recall she was having a famous time last night so I trust it does not appear serious.'

'I don't think so, but I am reluctant to take a chance on that. Even after I have physicked her with mercury water she is not at all improved.'

'It is always as well to receive professional advice, I always believe.'

'Oh, indeed, Lady Farrowdale.'

'You must allow me to summon my own physician. You will not be sorry even though his methods cannot be said to be orthodox.'

Caroline opened her mouth to refuse the offer but thought better of it; best encourage her favour whilst she may. Once the countess learned . . .

'It is kind of you to trouble.'

'It is no trouble. I would like to be of service to you if I may.'

Warming to her now Caroline asked, 'Lady Farrowdale, will you take a dish of tea with me?'

For the first time the lady smiled, and warmly too. 'No, my dear. This is not in the ordinary way of social calls so let us not mince words; I have come to congratulate you.'

Caroline frowned. 'Lady Farrowdale, forgive me but I do not understand.'

'I think you do, my dear. My husband paid a rather late call upon you last night, did he

44

not?'

Caroline's cheeks flamed. 'How could you know that, ma'am?'

'Quite simply because my dolt of a husband told me so himself.' Caroline could only stare at her in stupefaction. 'Yes, you may well look at me like that, but you may be sure he is treating the entire matter as a huge jest.'

'That . . . is a great, . . . relief,' Caroline answered, still somewhat bewildered by the countess's attitude.

'My dear, you must know you have my undying admiration. Farrowdale is deserving of your treatment, which is long overdue. For years the silly old fool has been throwing his cap over the windmill for any number of chits who were invariably stupid enough to succumb to his lovemaking. You are the first one to my knowledge to behave with any degree of sensibility. You are deserving of Lady Bleasedale's bracelet and I wish you joy of wearing it.'

'Oh, I could not possibly do that. I sent it round to her ladyship's house this morning—with Lord Farrowdale's compliments.'

At this the countess threw back her head and laughed heartily. 'My dear,' she said at last, wiping her eyes, 'that is famous. I am quite sure you will become all the rage before long.'

Caroline felt happier now, although still quite bewildered. The socialites of the *beau monde* had such odd attitudes, it was difficult for a newcomer to know what behaviour invited scorn and which created admiration. In this instance it seemed she had done precisely the right thing to increase her standing, but she needed no reminding of how easily quite the opposite effect could have been achieved.

'That is not my object, Lady Farrowdale. I would prefer to live quietly, much as I have always done, but I am here to see my sister settled.'

'You can rely upon me to be your ally in that, Lady Kilgarron. You and I shall be bosom friends from today onwards. I can assure you there will be no assembly to which you and Miss Winton will not be invited.'

Caroline took a deep breath. 'I am overwhelmed by your generosity, Lady Farrowdale.'

The countess rose majestically to her feet, glancing at Caroline again with a critical eye. 'You dress well, my dear. Very well for one who has rusticated so long. I have always patronised Madame Clemtier in Bond Street . . .'

'She has a wonderful reputation, but I could not aspire to such a mistress of the art. My own mantua-maker is Mademoiselle Floriste in The Strand. She is not as yet well-known but recently come from Paris.'

'She is exceeding well-known and will be even more so once you are seen abroad. You

46

may ask her to call on me. She is deserving of patronage.'

Caroline hurried after her. 'She will regard it as an honour, my lady, and so do I.'

Lady Farrowdale paused in the hall to receive her gloves from the footman. 'Have no further concern for Miss Winton. I will make sure Dr Thorne is here within the hour.'

'Your concern is so kind.'

'Not at all. I am sure we shall see a great deal of each other in the future. *Adieu*, my dear.'

For several minutes after the countess's departure Caroline could hardly think in a proper manner and then she began to laugh out loud, before running up the stairs to regale Polly with every detail of the conversation.

CHAPTER FOUR

'I cannot credit our good fortune,' Polly said when Caroline finished telling her tale. 'Such condescension on the part of her ladyship. But you should have told me what happened last night.'

'I had no wish to worry you. You see, I had no notion what the result would be. It seemed more like that Lord Farrowdale would tell no one, but would make certain we were socially unacceptable by way of revenge. It makes no odds any more, I am glad to say.'

'You will be notorious,' Polly warned, much to her sister's amusement.

'I own I do not mind in the least, if the result is to frighten off gentlemen like the earl.'

Polly gave her a curious look then. 'Why do you keep a pistol beneath your pillow?'

'Oh, because we are females living alone, and I had heard London was a dangerous place.' She was momentarily thoughtful. 'In any event it is as well that I did, for I have no wish to be at any man's mercy.'

Polly continued to look at her sister curiously for a moment or two before she winced and sank back into the pillows. Caroline was concerned again and it was fortuitous that a servant interrupted at that moment.

'A Dr Thorne has arrived, my lady, and says he is expected.'

Caroline immediately stood up. 'Have him shown up immediately.' She looked to her sister and smiled. 'Lady Farrowdale is as good as her word.'

Polly managed a wry grin. 'She is a very forceful lady whom no one would dare gainsay.'

'Only Lord Farrowdale,' her sister answered wryly.

'He and Lady Farrowdale seem to dislike each other heartily.'

'I am persuaded that is only outward appearances. I am quite convinced they are rather fond of each other.'

Polly sighed. 'At least whatever this Dr Thorne may prescribe cannot be worse than your mercury water, which is vile.'

Caroline hurried to the door as the physician was about to be shown in. There was a smile of welcome on her lips which soon turned to a look of surprise, for instead of the eminent and bewigged gentleman she had expected there stood the young man she had noticed at the Farrowdales' rout.

'Lady Kilgarron?'

She snapped out of her surprise as he looked at her curiously. 'Yes, yes,' she murmured.

'Jarrod Thorne. Lady Farrowdale informs

49

me you are in need of my services.'

Rather bemused Caroline nodded and ushered him towards the bed. 'My sister has been unwell all day. A dose of mercury water has had no effect.'

He had been gazing at the patient but now he looked to Caroline again, frowning slightly. 'Mercury water? You are most fortunate it has had no effect. I only wonder she is as well as she seems.'

Caroline stiffened at such blatant ridicule. 'It is a noted remedy, Dr Thorne.'

'A remedy for what, Lady Kilgarron? I have rarely seen it cure anything. It can certainly make an end to a person much more quickly than any ague. However, if you insist upon administering home remedies I would prefer you to use Daffy's Elixir. That, at least, does *nothing*.'

Caroline was hard-pressed to suppress her anger any longer and, noting it Polly said quickly, 'I recall you were at Lady Farrowdale's last night.'

He smiled then. 'Ah yes, it was generally held to be an excellent rout and I'll warrant we all ate and drank too much on that occasion. Do you feel very ill, Miss Winton?'

'Yes, indeed, and it is quite unlike me. We Wintons are as strong as farm horses, and rarely sicken.'

'Even horses do that sometimes,' he answered much to Polly's amusement.

50

'I only hope I haven't contracted a putrid fever. I am told they are exceeding rife in London.'

'No fever at all,' he answered, putting a light hand on her brow.

He looked at Caroline again. 'You have no cause for concern, Lady Kilgarron.'

'I am relieved to hear you say so,' she answered, none too pleased with his manner.

'I would recommend two days rest, and a diet only of beef broth.' He smiled at Polly. 'I'll call back at the end of that period. Good day to you, Miss Winton,' he added, bowing slightly.

Caroline walked back across the room at his side. 'Is that all you intend to do, Dr Thorne?'

'Nothing more is necessary, Lady Kilgarron. You will see the improvement in a day or so.' He glanced around. 'It is a trifle stuffy in here and it might be beneficial to Miss Winton if a window could be opened a fraction.'

'The London air is not held to be healthful,' Caroline protested.

He looked at her in mild surprise. 'I have been inhaling it all day with no ill-effect,' he answered and once again anger almost caused her to make a sharp retort.

He was quite blatantly insolent, which was an unfortunate vice in a doctor to fashionable society. Sir Edgar's physician had been quite a different kind of a man, a veritable toady, always anxious to please. Caroline would not

51

have wished Dr Thorne to be so anxious to grease her boots, but even so . . .

'You have prescribed no medicine. You have not even bled her.'

He paused by the door to look at her for a long, discomforting moment. 'You can be sure the malady is not in her blood, Lady Kilgarron.'

Breathlessly she asked, 'What does ail my sister? You have not said.'

'Nothing which need alarm you. I believe it is merely a case of over indulgence.'

Once again Caroline was taken aback. '*Over indulgence*, Dr Thorne? What manner of illness is that?'

He gave her a deprecating smile. 'A complaint rife in this city, ma'am, amongst certain sections of the population. Lady Farrowdale's cook uses a prodigious number of French sauces and spices which may irritate those unused to them. Your sister has fallen foul of a gastric protest.'

Caroline stiffened with indignation. 'I have never heard anything so outrageous, sir.'

He smiled again, wryly this time. 'The advice is yours to follow or disregard, Lady Kilgarron. A diet of only beef tea will soon put Miss Winton to rights but I cannot force you to accept my recommendations. You are perfectly at liberty to call in another physician who may advocate bleeding and purging.' He moved past her into the corridor and gave a little bow.

'Your servant, ma'am.'

Caroline watched him striding down the corridor and then she turned on her heel, stiff with anger. When she was once more in her sister's room she rang for a servant before saying, 'I really cannot conceive what Lady Farrowdale can be thinking of, sending that man to attend you.'

'I liked him. At least he did not wish to open a vein, and for that I cannot be sorry.'

'I am quite convinced the man is a mountebank. I'm going to send for Sir James.'

'No, Caro, I beg of you do not. I feel we should give his regime a chance to work.'

A maidservant came in answer to the summons, saying, 'You rang, my lady?'

'Please, Caro,' Polly begged. 'I do not want to be bled and purged—at least not yet.'

Her sister drew in a deep sigh. 'Ask Cook to prepare a dish of beef tea for Miss Winton.'

She turned then to smile at Polly. 'He had better not be in error in this matter.'

The girl chuckled. 'After Lord Farrowdale's experience with you last night, I doubt if anyone would dare cross you, Caro!'

*   *   *

Despite Caroline's lack of faith in Dr Thorne's odd regime, Polly was soon back in her usual high spirits. Although her sister was delighted this was so, she was slightly piqued too at his accurate diagnosis, and when it was time for him to call again she contrived to be elsewhere, leaving Beth to accompany him. In any event the call was merely a perfunctory one as Polly was now up on her feet again, anxious to take part in the hitherto busy social life.

'I am so relieved we can attend Lady Bleasedale's ball,' she confided in Caroline after Dr Thorne's visit.

'Only if you are certain you are up to it.'

'Oh, yes indeed, and I have learned my lesson, you may be sure. No more will I be tempted by so much food. After all, we have always eaten simply and sparingly. I am persuaded Dr Thorne is quite brilliant.'

'Oh, ' 'twas merely a fortunate incidence, Polly,' her sister said airily, continuing with her embroidery. 'I have little faith in his methods, so it is as well your malady was not a serious one. Had that been the case I am not at all convinced the outcome would have been as happy.'

'Well, I trust you will call him in again should I sicken in the future. I shall patronise him, you may be sure.'

Caroline bit back a sharp retort, for she knew she was being unfair. Instead she said, 'I noted several posies left for you in the hall whilst you were abed.'

The colour crept up Polly's cheeks. 'They were all from Mr Underwood.' Caroline looked up from her embroidery. 'He is very nice, don't you think?'

'As I am scarcely acquainted with the gentleman, Polly, I cannot say, but he does seem presentable. Do you like him?' she asked lightly, returning her attention to her embroidery.

Her sister nodded. 'More than anyone I have yet encountered in London.' Caroline's needle faltered and Polly went on. 'We have received an invitation from Mrs Underwood to a card party at her home in Bloomsbury Square. Shall we accept, Caro?'

The girl waited with baited breath until her sister answered in a careless tone, 'Yes, I believe we shall. We cannot afford to offend anyone as yet.'

Now Polly smiled happily. 'Indeed, but it is true you are very much in demand.'

'By a number of dowagers anxious to quiz me on our antecedents, and their rakish spouses who wish to become my lover. I am given to understand bets are being made on who will succeed. I hope they are prepared to lose their money.'

Polly giggled. 'Is there no one you favour?'

'Certainly not,' Caroline answered emphatically. 'Did you really think there would be?'

'Not as a lover, but perchance as a spouse. Not all men are married.'

'I have a measure of independence which I

never dreamed would be mine and I am in no mind to give that up.'

'Not even if you fell madly in love?' Polly ventured.

The needle pricked Caroline's thumb and she sucked it for a moment or two before answering. 'My love-life is not the object of our being here.'

Polly blushed again before saying in a carefully controlled voice, 'I believe Mr Underwood to be in earnest about me.'

Caroline did not answer for a moment or two and then she said, 'But dearest, we have scarce been here long enough.'

'Mr Underwood is not a rake. He is a most abstemious and serious-minded man. All the other bucks frighten me so, Caro. I am not in the least like you. If Lord Farrowdale had come into *my* bedchamber I know I should have died of fright.'

'That is beside the point. You have scarce had the opportunity to meet many eligible young men as yet. The Season is young and I am convinced you will fall in love many times before you make your final choice.'

'Do you really think so?' Polly asked doubtfully. 'What concerns me is that I have no aristocratic antecedents, unlike others of my acquaintance.'

'That is of no consequence.'

'It seems to be of the utmost interest to everyone else, who ask the most probing questions.'

'They may very well be interested—that is only natural—but I assure you it does not *matter*.'

'I'm persuaded everyone believes us to be well-connected and there are times when I feel a fraud.'

'We *are* well-connected,' Caroline told her with a laugh.

'You know very well what I mean.'

Caroline looked at her sympathetically then. 'We have never said anything to give rise to any speculation, Polly. We are accepted for what we are. I am sure you worry too much.'

It was her sister's turn to smile, although it was still a worried one. 'You are possibly right.' She frowned again. 'I know Mr Underwood would not be the brilliant match you had hoped for, but when the time comes—as it may—you would not refuse him out of hand, would you, Caro?'

She smiled reassuringly again. 'No, of course I would not, but I do ask that you take time to consider your future and not rush to throw your cap over the windmill.'

Polly gave her an eager nod and a smile and Caroline continued with her embroidery, not the least reassured.

CHAPTER FIVE

The card party at Mrs Underwood's house turned out to be a much more splendid affair than Caroline had envisaged, with almost as many people attending as had the Farrowdales' rout. For those who wished to eschew the card tables, dancing was provided, and Caroline noted that Thomas Underwood had once more bespoken many of the sets with Polly from the outset, something she viewed with mixed feelings.

Mrs Underwood was one of the least intimidating matrons of the *ton* and treated Caroline with great hospitality, which perhaps was not so surprising with the prospect of Polly's portion in view for her son.

It was also the first occasion on which Caroline had seen Lord Farrowdale since the night he had climbed up to her bedchamber, and she was naturally apprehensive. However, no one, much less the earl himself, behaved as if anything was amiss and there were sufficient people present to obviate any awkwardness.

Caroline decided at the outset she would opt to play cards rather than accept invitations to the dance, which would probably eliminate any awkwardness and avoid a repetition of that incident. For a while she watched Polly dancing a gavotte with Mr Underwood whom she had to own was a presentable young man with no apparent vices, unusual enough she thought, in any kind of society much less this one.

'They are becoming inseparable,' Lady Bleasedale commented as she came up to Caroline.

Caroline cast her a faint smile. 'So it would seem.'

She was glad to note that this lady was once again wearing her diamond and emerald bracelet. Caroline hoped she would not be foolish enough to wager such a precious possession again, but she really doubted it. Caroline had good reason to know that many people gambled until nothing was left and only promissary notes could be offered.

Lady Bleasedale was looking at her speculatively now. 'You are very young to act merely as your sister's chaperon,' she ventured a moment later. 'This Season could very well see you settled too.'

Caroline did not doubt that there would be a great deal of speculation on that score, but she answered unequivocally, 'Polly is my prime concern, Lady Bleasedale. I cannot think of anything beyond her welfare.'

'How commendable. You are a very remarkable young lady.'

'That is precisely my opinion,' said the Countess of Farrowdale, who had come up to them unseen.

Accompanying her was a good-looking young man of about Caroline's own age. He was gazing at her with an admiration she was only just becoming accustomed to. As she gave him a perfunctory smile she thought fleetingly that he reminded her of someone, but the connection eluded her.

Lady Bleasedale wandered away into the crowd and the other woman said, 'Allow me to introduce my son, Lady Kilgarron. Viscount Sanderton, the eldest of my,' laughingly now, 'considerable brood.'

The young man bowed low over Caroline's hand. 'Your servant, ma'am.'

'I am delighted to make your acquaintance, Lord Sanderton.'

He smiled again. 'Be assured the honour is all mine, ma'am.' He subjected her to yet another admiring look before saying, 'Your team of greys is eliciting a deal of attention, Lady Kilgarron. May I ask who advises you in the purchase of your cattle?'

'Certainly you may, Lord Sanderton. I chose them myself.'

The young man looked startled as Caroline knew he would. 'My lady, that is indeed remarkable. You have an excellent eye.'

She smiled from behind her fan. 'I shall not deny it.'

'May I ask how you came by such an excellent eye?'

Her eyes were sparkling with amusement.

'My father was in some small way an expert, my lord, and in the absence of having a son taught me all I know.'

'Incredible,' he breathed, and then, 'Would you do me the honour of standing up with me later in the evening?'

Suddenly Caroline realised who he reminded her of—very strongly too. Dr Thorne. The realisation shook her and she looked to Lady Farrowdale in a startled way which fortunately she did not notice.

'Lady Kilgarron?' the young man was asking.

She returned her attention to him once more. 'Yes, I would like that, Lord Sanderton,' she answered absently.

'Then be pleased to excuse me for now; I am engaged for this set.'

He bowed again and as he walked away Caroline watched him go. She knew full well that by-blows were often brought up as legitimate off-spring but she had never knowingly encountered the phenomenon before.

'He has been longing to make your acquaintance,' his mother said and Caroline gave her her attention once again.

'He is a fine young man. You must be very proud of him.'

The countess smiled. 'Indeed I am. He is not so wild as some, I am glad to say, but a bright young blade for all that he favours his father.'

Caroline could only smile to herself at that observation and was on her way to the card room to play picquet some time later when she came face to face with Jarrod Thorne himself.

She felt somewhat uncomfortable but gave him a faint smile and would have gone on with no further ado if he had not said, 'Good evening to you, Lady Kilgarron. I notice Miss Winton is fully recovered from her indisposition.'

His swaggering assurance only served to irritate her anew but she managed to say in a civil tone, 'Happily that is so, and she seems to believe it is due to your regime entirely.'

He inclined his head slightly and there was a light of amusement in his eyes which she did not miss. 'You obviously do not share her opinion.'

'On the contrary, Dr Thorne, I am mightily obliged to you. You have my wholehearted gratitude.'

If he recognised the gentle mockery in her voice he gave no sign of it. He merely answered, 'You too have earned everyone's admiration.' She looked at him curiously. 'To have bested Lord Farrowdale is an achievement indeed.'

She stiffened at the reminder of how widespread was the discussion of that incident. 'There must be few enough people who are not aware of what happened.'

'Are you surprised, Lady Kilgarron? Such an incident is rare enough; that it should happen to this Season's most noteworthy female is an added bonus.'

Caroline felt acutely discomforted. 'As the business does not reflect well upon him I am only surprised he boasts of it.'

'He is an old reprobate as everyone knows, but he is not in the least ill-natured which is fortunate for you, my lady.'

His eyes narrowed slightly as he looked past her and when Caroline turned she was horrified to see Lord Farrowdale himself approaching.

'Now, now, Thorne, you charlatan, don't think you can keep Lady Kilgarron all to yourself. Go fawn upon all the old matrons who pay your fees with such alacrity.'

'Lady Kilgarron has gladly paid my fee, and I recall you did not call me a charlatan when I cured you of the ague.'

'Well, I tell you I intend to engage Lady Kilgarron for this next set.'

Although Caroline was delighted to see him in such good spirits she had no intention of inviting speculation or his odious attentions by standing up with him.

'Lord Farrowdale, I do not intend to stand up at all this evening.' She smiled. 'I have been rather tired of late and wish only to play picquet this evening.'

'Tired!' he bellowed, much to her

discomfort. 'Did you hear that, Thorne? What would you recommend, eh? A cupping? A blister mayhap. If you miss this opportunity you are not the man I believe you to be.'

The younger man looked amused. 'Dare I suggest a good night's rest?'

Lord Farrowdale looked startled and Caroline answered, 'Thank you, Dr Thorne. Mayhap I shall one day take your advice upon that.'

So saying she took her leave of them, feeling relieved to do so. Each man in his own way tended to disconcert her. The ladies of the *ton*, however, playing picquet in an anteroom held no terrors for her. Even their never-ending questions did not dismay her, for she had arrived in London well prepared for any that might be asked.

Several ladies were already seated and hard at play. Caroline soon found herself partnered with the Duchess of Darnley, a rather over-painted and elaborately dressed lady, but nevertheless an influential one. Nearby others were playing loo, and there was a great deal of noise emanating from those around the faro table.

The duchess quizzed Caroline thoroughly through her glass before they began to play their cards. Caroline was not an expert but she felt she could acquit herself respectably and knew anyway it would not do, to trounce so influential a lady as the duchess.

'So you are the young lady of whom I have heard so much,' the duchess said at last as she played her trick.

'I do not doubt it, your grace,' Caroline replied demurely, 'although I cannot conceive why I am of the least interest to anyone.'

The duchess gave a short, sharp laugh. 'Can you not? Ha! What a lark.' She raised her quizzing glass again. 'Your diamonds are quite splendid, my dear. Are they Winton diamonds or Kilgarron jewels?'

'Kilgarron, your grace. My family, respectable as they are, do not have the means to purchase such jewels.'

The duchess laughed again. 'I like your style, girl. Indeed I do.'

Caroline drew an almost indiscernible sigh of relief and the duchess frowned at her then. 'You are, no doubt, of the Buckinghamshire Wintons. I recall their pockets were always to let.'

Caroline smiled slightly as she ostensibly studied her cards. 'No, your grace; the Gloucestershire Wintons as a matter of fact.'

The duchess quizzed her again, the cards momentarily forgotten. 'I am not acquainted with them.'

'That does not surprise me to any degree, your grace; we led a very quiet life.'

'You did not have a Season, I am sure.'

'Sir Edgar made an offer for me before one could be arranged.'

The duchess smiled then. 'I own I cannot blame him, my dear.'

'What a romantic story,' murmured another lady who was sitting close by and listening to all that was being said. 'And even more so due to the tragic ending.'

'Miss Winton's Season appears to be a success in any event,' the duchess continued, playing her cards once more.

'It could not be more so, your grace,' Caroline answered, 'which is a very gratifying instance, I must own.'

'There is no secret about the way things are moving, and I can tell you that the Underwoods are a perfectly good family, if unremarkable. I trust that does not disturb you.'

'My sister's happiness is my prime concern, your grace.'

'A very admirable sentiment too. Miss Winton does not, I warrant, realise how fortunate she is in being able to choose her own partner. I was informed by my father who it was I must marry. There was no thought of objecting even had I wished to do so, as is so often the case with today's young people.'

'That was true of my marriage also,' Caroline told her, studying her cards carefully. 'I had no choice in the matter.'

'Not that it comes amiss,' the duchess amended. 'My own marriage has been perfectly happy. Young gals tend to throw their caps over the windmill for any young blade with a small amount of address. They don't always know what is best for them.'

Caroline had to smile. 'But they often know what is *not* best for them, your grace.'

The duchess looked at her in surprise and then began to laugh, joined by several other ladies nearby.

'Lady Kilgarron has considerable wit,' another of the ladies said.

'My dear,' the duchess told her, 'there will be many a gentleman in pursuit of you, so you had best keep that pistol about you if you are not inclined to take a lover.'

Caroline smiled wryly. 'I have every intention of doing so, you grace.'

'Why are you so resistant to. their charms?' one lady asked. 'It is something which puzzles me greatly.'

'I am quite recently widowed,' Caroline told her by way of explanation.

The lady continued to look bewildered. 'I cannot see the connection. One thing has little to do with another.'

'Perhaps it is just that the gentleman in question is not quite to Lady Kilgarron's taste,' someone said slyly. 'Such fastidiousness is always to be admired if not quite understood.'

Caroline was beginning to feel uncomfortable when the duchess looked up, saying, 'Dr Thorne, I had no notion you were interested in picquet. Do you intend to join us in play?'

It gave Caroline something of a start to realise Jarrod Thorne was standing a little way behind her chair, watching the game. It was possible he had been there for some time, no doubt listening to their conversation too. He smiled slightly in the undemonstrative way which quietly impressed her.

'No, your grace, I think not. Picquet, I have always considered, more of a ladies' game and I would not encroach upon that.'

The duchess laughed gruffly. 'How wise of you. We would soon relieve you of your purse.'

'That is exactly my fear, your grace, so if you will excuse me . . .'

He bowed and wandered towards the faro table. Caroline watched him go, a singular figure in his dark, broadcloth coat which on other men would look dowdy but somehow had the effect of making him appear the more elegant.

Moreover, he always seemed so aloof from the rest of the guests at these functions. Caroline could understand it, however. He was not present to be diverted, but merely to keep in touch with those wealthy and influential people who would be glad to pay his fee whenever illness overtook them.

'My game, I think,' the duchess said, claiming Caroline's attention once more. 'Are you acquainted with Dr Thorne, Lady Kilgarron?'

'Er, yes, yes I am. My sister was unwell earlier this week and Lady Farrowdale was gracious enough to recommend Dr Thorne to attend her.'

''Tis obvious she is recovered,' one of the other players remarked.

Out of the corner of her eye Caroline noticed that he was now in conversation with Lady Farrowdale's pretty young daughter, who had also made her debut that Season. They were conversing and laughing together with remarkable ease and it was obvious the Farrowdale girl found him not the least discomforting to be with.

'She is quite well now,' Caroline answered, returning her attention to her companions, 'although I take leave to doubt whether Dr Thorne's treatment is the cause of it.'

'Do you not consider him suitable then?' someone asked.

'I think it is rather a case of disliking his manner,' Caroline answered carefully.

'Oh, he is not in the least obsequious, but he is well-qualified, I believe,' one of the ladies told her. 'A fellow of the Royal Society by all accounts and Lady Farrowdale told me he has even studied anatomy in Edinburgh with a man called . . . ah, yes, Tertius.' She laughed. 'Such a strange name and it always stays in my mind. Of course,' she added, 'I have the utmost faith in Sir James Eversleigh and I doubt if anyone could prevail upon me to change my mind on that score.'

'Nonsense,' the duchess snapped. 'I can speak of Dr Thorne's ability with sure knowledge. When my own dear Hector was ill—and I was prepared to see him off within the sen'night you may know—Dr Thorne advised me to give him foxglove tea of all things. I thought that young man had taken leave of his senses, but sure enough the foxglove tea effected a cure. Now, whenever an attack comes on, I make a cupful and Hector is very soon better.'

Caroline was, despite herself, impressed and more so when one of the younger ladies added, 'Indeed, I must agree with her grace on this occasion. When my poor little James sickened some time ago Dr Thorne exhorted me to throw off his swaddling bands, open up the nursery windows and give him goats milk several times a day. Nurse almost had a seizure and predicted all manner of dire results, but poor James was so ill I would as lief do anything, and he is now,' she beamed, 'the healthiest child imaginable.' The woman looked earnestly at Caroline. 'When a son is the first after five girls, my dear, one is desperate to do *anything* to save him.'

Caroline murmured her agreement. The cards, it seemed, were forgotten as the ladies indulged in a far more enjoyable coze.

'Even so, Lady Farrowdale seems inordinately keen on Dr Thorne,' Caroline ventured a moment later, 'and in truth I cannot conceive why she should patronise him so heavily.'

There was a moment's pause before the others began to laugh merrily, causing Caroline to look at them in some dismay.

'I do beg your pardon. Have I said something amusing?'

'Do you truly not know the connection between the two?' asked one of the others.

Caroline shook her head whilst the laughter continued and then her cheeks grew more pink. 'Oh, indeed. I believe I do understand,' she murmured, recalling her introduction to Lady Farrowdale's eldest son. 'Lady Farrowdale and Dr Thorne must be . . . lovers.'

The duchess contrived to look heartily amused. 'That could well be, my dear. We cannot say for certain, but what is true is the fact that Dr Thorne is Lady Farrowdale's brother in law.' Caroline stared at her uncomprehendingly. 'He is the earl's youngest brother.'

'Now you *are* gammoning me.'

'No, indeed, dear,' one of the others assured her. 'Thorne is indeed Lord Farrowdale's brother. Thorne is their family name. In fact Farrowdale is exceeding fond of telling everyone his ancestor was the "Thorne" in Cromwell's side. I am surprised you have not heard that yourself.'

Caroline smiled in a bewildered way. 'I

cannot credit the connection. They are not in the least alike. I cannot think of two men more unalike.'

The duchess began to deal the cards. 'No one would argue with the validity of that statement. It is nevertheless true.'

Caroline still felt stunned, for it was the last thing she expected to hear. She could not have imagined Jarrod Thorne as Lady Farrowdale's lover, but even that would have been more logical.

'Of course,' the duchess went on, 'there are good number of years between the two, Farrowdale being the eldest and Thorne the youngest of a large family. It's an Irish title, you know, and not one overendowed with fortune. In fact, I believe there were a number of sisters to settle, leaving little for Dr Thorne who was obliged to seek his own way in the world. Farrowdale came by his fortune when he married Augusta who is the only daughter of the Marquis of Frampton. The marriage was frowned upon by her family, but I recall well that she would have no one else.' The duchess looked at Caroline. 'Farrowdale has a deal of charm when he chooses to exert it as you have no doubt discovered,' she added to Caroline's further discomposure.

'I am obliged to you all for the information,' she told them with a smile. 'I should have hated to commit a *faux pas* because of my ignorance of the facts.'

'You will soon become *au fait* with all the *on dits*, my dear,' she was told.

Caroline smiled her appreciation but a moment later ventured, 'I note that Dr Thorne's wife is not present tonight.'

'He is not wed,' the duchess answered, 'although no doubt he will emulate his brother and marry an heiress. He must needs do so otherwise marriage would be a shabby affair for him.'

Caroline looked up from her cards. 'I understood that physicians received considerable incomes from their fees. The fee I paid to Dr Thorne was a generous one, I might add.'

'Sir James Eversleigh is as rich as Croesus,' someone answered, 'and with Augusta Farrowdale's patronage Dr Thorne is set to emulate him, but as Augusta herself was bemoaning to me only the other day, he spends every penny he earns on his Dispensary for the Poor in Cannon Lane.' The woman looked at the duchess. 'Your grace, have you yet visited it?'

The duchess, intent upon her cards, shook her head, causing several powdered curls to fall loose. 'No, although I am given to believe it is uncommonly interesting.'

'It is certainly an excellent place for the poor to come when they are ill, but in my opinion Dr Thorne exhibits the greatest eccentricity in spending the greater part of his time there.'

'How else are the poor to be treated?' Caroline asked. 'They cannot afford a physician's fees.'

'There are many physicians who are able to do such good work, my dear, but Dr Thorne has an excellent entree into the most exclusive circles through his family connections.' The woman looked at her companions then. ''Tis the most remarkable place for all that it is in a rundown area of the Town. Everything is actually *scrubbed* frequently including the patients, one of his helpers told me. Your grace must certainly find the time to go. It is, of course, encouraged that we should do so. Dr Thorne relies upon our bounty for the existence of this place, but your grace would enjoy the anatomising, I know.'

At this the duchess looked up. 'Dr Thorne is not as far as I am aware a surgeon, Lady Newton.'

'But he anatomises bodies, your grace, in order to determine why they have died.'

'That is a useless exercise if the creature is already dead,' one lady commented with a laugh.

'But, if a cause is found,' Caroline explained, 'it may help some other person suffering from alike disease.'

The duchess's eyes were agleam, the cards once more forgotten. 'Anatomising, you say? How very interesting. Yes, indeed, Lady

Newton, a visit to this dispensary sounds most interesting. I shall make a point of visiting it as soon as time permits.'

Caroline gave her a wry look, never failing to marvel at the pleasures of these well-bred ladies, which varied from the enjoyment and patronage of good music and drama, to the witnessing of the flogging of lunatics in Bedlam, the hanging of criminals at Tyburn and, most enjoyable of all, the dissecting of the bodies at the Surgeon's Hall.

Caroline herself knew she could find no such pleasure in these sights, but there was no doubt her curiosity was aroused by Jarrod Thorne and she too determined she would visit the Cannon Lane Dispensary for the Poor as soon as she was able.

The conversation was brought to an end by the announcement that refreshments were about to be served.

The duchess threw her cards on the table and Caroline paid her losses which were small in comparison to others.

'It has been a pleasure to play a hand with you, my dear,' she was told. 'You and Miss Winton shall have an invitation to my musical soiree next month.'

Caroline flushed with pleasure. 'We shall look forward to it, your grace.'

'Ah, here is Lord Trumble to give you his arm into supper, no doubt.' She laughed. 'I do not suppose he has come to escort *me*. Even

Darnley does not do that any more.'

Caroline smiled at the Marquis of Trumble and allowed him to escort her to the supper room. She immediately glanced around in the hope of seeing Polly, fully expecting her to be with Thomas Underwood, so it came as a great shock when she finally caught sight of her sister—not with the moonstruck clergyman, but with Jarrod Thorne, and Polly was conversing with him as if she had known him all her life.

CHAPTER SIX

Despite her decision to do so, Caroline soon forgot her wish to visit Dr Thorne's dispensary except on those occasions when his presence at some social function reminded her. In fact she scarcely had time to pause for breath, for so many invitations were delivered to their house and, of course, she was determined to accept as many of them as possible.

Many married noblemen still attempted to become her lover, although none of them went as far as Lord Farrowdale in order to achieve their desires once Caroline had made it quite clear she was not interested in their attentions. Just as many unmarried men proposed marriage, and some of them were very eligible indeed. Although she was flattered she gave not one of them cause to hope.

Her refusal to respond to courtship was not merely because she was not in love with any of them. At twenty she was no older than many of the girls seeking husbands during the current Season, but the difference was that she had already been married. The year as Sir Edgar's wife might well have been only a short time but it served to mature Caroline to a great degree—she realised this more than ever now—and simply, all those men who sought her hand seemed too young. Of course the older ones were invariably married.

Flattered and amused by their ardour, Caroline nevertheless wished more gentlemen would pursue Polly. It was her Season, the very reason they had come to London at all. But Polly continued to favour Mr Underwood with the result that any other young man displaying a partiality very soon lost interest.

Polly invariably stood up to dances with the clergyman and Caroline was just beginning to be resigned to the inevitable result when it suddenly became apparent that there might be another suitor in the offing—Jarrod Thorne.

Ever since the night of Mrs Underwood's card party, Caroline had become increasingly aware that Jarrod Thorne was showing a marked interest in her sister. Even more surprising, Polly was far from indifferent to him. She stood up on occasions to dance with him—as indeed Caroline herself had done several times. Caroline would not have worried about it at all, except that Polly felt at ease with so few people, previously confining herself almost exclusively to Mr Underwood.

Caroline could not understand her sister's attitude, for she herself still found Jarrod Thorne the most discomforting man. The way he looked at her was not in the least adoring or admiring and yet it was not dispassionate either; amused and knowing was perhaps more like the truth and it definitely had the effect of disconcerting her as nothing else could do.

What irked Caroline most was something the Duchess of Darnley had said. Dr Thorne must needs wed an heiress and Polly had a fair portion to her name. The fact that her sister should be pursued solely on this account did not please Caroline at all.

It remained, however, that both sisters were enjoying themselves hugely for the first time in their lives and on that score alone Caroline refused to worry about anything, until one bright, spring morning, that is, when she returned from an early ride in the Park. She paused to look through the cards and letters which had arrived that day and she stiffened to find a letter from France amongst them. It was addressed to her at Kilgarron Manor, but had been forwarded to London from there. After reading it quickly Caroline was even less pleased but was immediately diverted when Polly came down the stairs.

'Good morning, dearest! How you put me to shame by being up and abroad so early.'

Caroline managed to smile, despite the misgivings teasing her thoughts. 'I do not sleep as well as you. You are bright and happy this morning, I am glad to note.'

'Oh, it is going to be a wonderful day. I feel it in my bones.'

Caroline gave her an indulgent look. 'You had a very diverting time last night, did you not?'

Polly nodded. 'It was sublime.'

'You are becoming quite the socialite, my dear.'

'As you are oft exhorting me, I am making the most of this Season. Tomorrow I may awake and find myself back at Kilgarron Manor.'

A hard look came into Caroline's eyes then. 'That is something which will never happen.'

Then Polly giggled. 'Oh, did you see Mr Underwood's face when Dr Thorne engaged me for two sets?'

Her sister gave her a cold look. 'He was understandably out of countenance. You are becoming quite a minx, Polly. You will be gaining a reputation as a flirt if you do not take care.'

'You did tell me to associate more with different gentlemen before I choose my spouse.'

Caroline stiffened and then she asked with studied carelessness, 'Does Dr Thorne come into the reckoning now?'

'He always makes me feel at ease when I am overwhelmed by the company we are in but he has given me no reason to expect an offer, and even if he did my heart still belongs to Mr Underwood. I am not a flirt, Caro. I couldn't be if I tried.'

Her sister turned away to hide the relief now evident on her face. 'I am glad to hear it, for I am persuaded Dr Thorne is no more than a fortune hunter.'

Polly looked dismayed. 'I am sure he must be quite rich from his fees.'

'Possibly, if he kept them, but his work at his Dispensary for the Poor eats well into his income, so there would be no money left to spend on bonnets and ribbons, or indeed even to support a wife in a modest manner.'

Polly's countenance fell. 'Even if that were so it would not dismay me. I have no illusions, Caro. I am not like you. No gentleman would marry me if it were not for my portion.'

'Polly . . .' Caroline began to protest, feeling distressed at the turn of the conversation.

'I do not doubt Mr Underwood's devotion, though. He truly has regard for me and all I ask, Caro, is a man who loves me and is kind.'

Caroline's face relaxed into a smile. 'Be assured that is all I want for you too, dearest.'

She felt nothing but relief although irrationally she could not understand why, given the choice, her sister preferred the insignificant Thomas Underwood to the dark, good looks of Jarrod Thorne.

'What do you have there in your hand?' Polly asked a moment later, taking her sister by surprise. 'Another invitation, perchance? Oh, do let me see it?'

Caroline had quite forgotten the letter in her hand, and before she could say, 'It is nothing of importance,' Polly had taken it from her.

She glanced at it. 'Why, it is from Mr

Brandon, in Paris!' she cried, going on to read it eagerly. Then she stiffened with indignation. 'Of all the impudence, Caroline! To ask you for money. I should send him away with a flea in his ear!'

'Don't use such vulgar expressions, Polly,' Caroline retorted irritably. 'It is not seemly for a girl of good breeding.'

Suitably chastened, Polly murmured, 'I do beg your pardon. I do forget myself at times.'

'Not in front of Mr Underwood, I trust,' she answered with a laugh, which made her sister grin.

'I do occasionally, but even ladies of Quality do sometimes utter surprising vulgarities.

'I own that it has surprised me too.'

Polly's amusement faded. 'All the same, this letter is an impudence.'

Caroline took it from her and went across the hall, still clad in her riding habit. 'Fudge! Mr Brandon has simply found himself embarrassed in Paris. I could not in all conscience ignore his plea.'

'You surely cannot intend to send him some money.'

'Just as small amount to tide him over. Tis of no consequence. We must remember he is, after all, Sir Edgar's cousin,' she added, smiling at her sister.

Polly's face relaxed into a smile too. 'You are far too good-natured, but I suppose I am a trifle prejudiced against him. I never did like

Mr Brandon with his mincing ways, you see.'

'I shall send him some money and then forget all about him. I trust that he will allow us to do so, for he will not find me so generous on another occasion, you may be certain. I am not what Father would have called a rum cull.

'Let us have breakfast and then we can go to the bank together.'

Polly looked immediately dismayed. 'Oh, I quite forgot to tell you; Mrs Underwood asked if I would like to visit the Zoo this morning.'

Caroline gave her a wry smile. 'No doubt Mr Underwood will be present too.'

'And one of the Devonshire girls too,' her sister added with a rare eagerness. 'May I go, Caro?'

'Of course you may. A visit to the bank cannot compare!' she added with a laugh.

*   *   *

Caroline came out of the dim exterior of the bank, blinking in the sunlight. She drew a slight sigh, knowing that a bill of exchange was now on its way to Paris. Hopefully no more would be heard of Mr Charles Brandon, whom Caroline liked no more than her sister, but deep within her she feared that this would not be so.

Several carriages were waiting at the kerbside and a great deal of activity was going on all around, mainly barrels of beer being delivered to the ale house which was situated a few yards away from the bank.

Her own footman was waiting to help her into the carriage and after that momentary hesitation, Caroline stepped up into it.

'Where to, my lady?' asked the driver a few moments later when she gave no directions.

The truth was that Caroline had no notion where she would go. The day was still young and for once she had no engagements until the evening. Suddenly she caught sight of a street sign. Cannon Lane. The name was familiar and jarred her memory. Then the connection came to her belatedly and she sat forward in the seat.

'Take me to the Cannon Lane Dispensary,' she ordered.

The driver gave her an odd look, but nevertheless set off immediately. The dispensary was situated only a few minutes away in an alley off Cannon Lane, a not very salubrious part of the town, where creatures lurked in doorways, their eyes bleak and their skins pale and pitted. Caroline was tempted then to turn back but she had never lacked courage and did not after all give the order to return.

The dispensary appeared to be nothing more than a shed which Caroline regarded askance for a moment or two before deciding to climb down.

Beth, her maid, was dismayed. 'You surely

do not intend to go in there, my lady.'

'I am curious to see this place,' she answered. 'I might even decide to become a patron if I am impressed.'

'You can do that well enough without exposing yourself to danger. There is bound to be contagion in there, ma'am, and I do beg of you to reconsider.'

'You may stay here if you choose, Beth, but I shall most certainly go in.'

'Oh no, ma'am, I could not, in all conscience, allow you to go in there unattended.'

However, the maidservant did hold back and it was Caroline who pushed open the door. She did not know what she expected to find, certainly not the crowd of people pressed into the large room she found herself in. All of them were poorly dressed, if not in rags. Coughing was a cacophony of noise equalled only by the crying of children and babies. Eyes filled with misery surveyed Caroline in her finery as she hesitated in the doorway before Beth finally went forward to make a way through the crowd.

'Out of the way there. Let my mistress through.'

She looked to her mistress for confirmation to go on and, somewhat more hesitant now, Caroline nodded grimly. Beth opened a door at the far side of the room which led to a much smaller one. As she went in Caroline hesitated in the doorway, taking in the scene before her and her eyes opened wide.

She had few preconceived ideas about what she would find at the dispensary, but certainly nothing like this scene of treatment being administered. At that moment Caroline realised how sheltered her life—and others like her—had been up until then.

A cry of agony filled the air causing Caroline to flinch but pride alone would not allow her to turn away as Beth was doing. A huge negro woman, bigger than any man Caroline had known, was attempting to hold down a man who was writhing on a table whilst Jarrod Thorne attempted to put what was obviously a badly broken leg into a splint.

'Hold him tighter, damn you, Nell!' he cried. 'Give him more brandy if you must, but keep him still!'

'Come my lady, this is no place for you,' Beth urged. 'We shall return later.'

'Later will make no odds, Beth. We shall only witness a similar scene, I fear. I am not in the least squeamish,' she added, still watching the painful procedure.

Jarrod Thorne paused momentarily to glance in her direction before returning to what seemed an impossible task. As soon as he attempted to put the splint in place, the man howled in pain and jerked away from the negro woman.

'By gad, the leg will have to go, Sam, if you

don't keep still!'

The negress continued to pour brandy down his throat in an effort to deaden the pain whilst a woman who had been holding clean bandages at the ready, wiped sweat off his brow.

Caroline came forward at last. 'It would be quicker to knock him senseless, I think.'

They all looked at her except for the wretched patient who was beginning to succumb to the effects of the brandy.

The negress grinned to reveal large, white teeth. 'That is what I keep tellin' 'im, ma'am. Yes, indeed I do.'

Jarrod Thorne was breathless from the effort of trying to splint the leg and he wiped the sweat off his own brow with his sleeve. 'We shall bear that in mind for another time, my lady. Now be pleased to step aside.'

Ignoring his request, she went on, 'I once saw a man thrown from a horse. He too broke a limb as badly as this one. My father knocked him senseless and splinted the limb before he could recover. The man neither died nor lost his leg,' she added proudly.

'Your *father?*' he asked in amazement.

She looked at him at last. 'In the country doctors are not always available. We often have to rely upon our own resources. We are not so fortunate as the people of Cannon Lane.'

He gave her a long look before glancing at

the patient again. 'I believe he is ready now and will be insensible to any pain. Mrs Anders would you show Lady Kilgarron around the dispensary?'

'Oh, I don't wish to incommode you, Dr Thorne . . .' Caroline protested.

He gently straightened the broken limb which elicited only a groan from the injured man, whereupon Caroline felt she could breathe again.

'On the contrary,' Dr Thorne replied, 'I am gratified that a lady with so many calls upon her time has graced us with her presence.'

Caroline stared at him, not knowing if there was any irony in the words, seemingly uttered with such sincerity.

Mrs Anders immediately put down the bandages and said, 'If you would come this way, Lady Kilgarron . . .'

She was small and slim, neatly and cleanly dressed, which was not what Caroline had expected from all she had heard about drunken and filthy nurses, certainly not this type of person who was altogether too refined.

Rather reluctantly, Caroline followed her into a large room with a high ceiling. The room was filled with people lying on truckle beds, set close together so that the maximum number could be accommodated.

'These are the patients who need continuous care and are too ill to go home—if they have one,' Mrs Anders told her.

'Why do they not go to a proper hospital?' Caroline asked, glancing around at the surprising neatness and lack of filth.

'Hospitals frighten them, ma'am. They fear they will not come out alive.'

'With good reason, I believe.'

'The man you have just seen is a case in point, ma'am. He was knocked into the gutter by a carriage this morning in Cheapside. Someone suggested he be taken to St Bartholomew's, but there they would have cut off his leg with no further ado, and the man was not too far gone to realise it. He managed to convey his wish to be brought here to those attempting to help him. Here he will stay and rest until the leg mends.'

'If it does,' Caroline interpolated, rather peevishly as she already knew it was possible to mend a broken limb.

'It is like he will not even limp,' Mrs Anders told her, not slow to rise to the challenge. 'Dr Thorne is a great believer in the theories of Dr Potts, who does not hold with amputating a limb if it can possibly be mended.'

'Well, I hope he may be right,' Caroline murmured, none the less impressed by what she had seen and heard so far.

Mrs Anders showed her into a room similar to the one they had just left but even more crowded with truckle beds.

'Do you nurse people with the pox and other such contagions?' Caroline asked, a mite uncomfortably.

'No, we must needs leave that to others, although Dr Thorne is very anxious to prevent an outbreak taking place. No doubt he has already explained it to you.'

Caroline did not like to admit he had not.

'If only we had room for more,' Mrs Anders complained from the heart a moment later. 'Dr Thorne has performed miracles with people who are all but dead when they arrive here. Just warmth, food and a clean bed can sometimes be enough, ma'am.'

Caroline did not miss the impassioned way she spoke and the use of the term 'we', and for the first time she began to look at her curiously.

'Have you been here long, Mrs Anders?'

The woman coloured somewhat, as if aware of her own excess of zeal. 'Two years, ma'am.'

'You must tell me how a person such as yourself came to be involved with this place. You are married, I note, so does your husband not object?'

The woman flushed again. 'I am a widow, ma'am.'

'So am I, Mrs Anders, so we are alike in that.'

The woman gave her a faint smile. 'That is the only similarity, ma'am. My husband was a schoolmaster. One day on his way home he was crushed beneath a curricle, which was being raced by a young blood. It had gone out of control.'

'That is a great misfortune,' Caroline told her, touched by the tale of tragedy.

'Your concern is too good, ma'am, but I am very fortunate when compared with most of the people who find themselves here.'

'Quite so, but that does not explain why you are here.'

'A few weeks after my husband died, our son, Joe, took ill with an ague. I feared he would die too and I had no money to call in a physician, but someone directed me to this place. Following Dr Thorne's directions I nursed Joe here for a sen'night. Mercifully he recovered and I was so impressed by what I saw, I offered my services to Dr Thorne.'

'You tell an impressive tale, Mrs Anders,' Caroline told her. 'Dr Thorne is fortunate in having your help and your devotion.'

'No, Lady Kilgarron,' she said, leading Caroline back the way they had come, 'I cannot hold with that. Joe and I are the fortunate ones. We have a home here now and I tend the sick gladly. In addition Dr Thorne pays me a small stipend to wash the bed-linen and keep the bandages clean, something which he is very anxious about.'

'I see. Tell me, Mrs Anders,' she said thoughtfully, 'is the blackamoor's story a similar one to yours?'

Mrs Anders laughed. 'No, indeed, ma'am. It could not be more different. Nell was brought back from the plantations in the Indies by her master who put her into . . . well,' she said, averting her eyes, 'you would not know of such places, ma'am.'

Caroline straightened her cuffs unnecessarily. 'On the contrary, I am well aware of the places to which you refer; my late husband, you see, was often a visitor to such an establishment.'

Mrs Anders was understandably taken-aback and then she said, 'I had forgotten how plain-spoken the Quality can be.'

Caroline smiled to herself before she prompted, 'You were telling me about the blackamoor. Pray continue if you will.'

Although Mrs Anders looked acutely discomforted she did as she was bid. 'When Nell was taken ill she was of no more use and thrown into the street to die, only some kind soul took pity on her and brought her here. Once she had recovered she was free to go, as such is the law on slaves in England, but where could she go, ma'am? She had nowhere. She stayed and is Dr Thorne's devoted servant. Her strength as you have seen today is of great value.'

'She is not the only one who is devoted, Mrs Anders,' Caroline pointed out and the other woman's cheeks grew red.

'You will, of course, wish to see the anatomising room,' she went on a little breathlessly a moment later.

'I think not,' Caroline answered absently.

Mrs Anders then looked at her curiously. 'But every visitor we've ever had is anxious to go there.'

Caroline did not doubt it. 'I have seen where the sick are healed. That is all which really interests me, Mrs Anders.'

The woman looked surprised as she ushered Caroline back into the room where the man with the broken leg was still lying on the table. Insensible still, although he groaned from time to time, Caroline noted that the leg was neatly splinted with clean bandages.

Apart from Nell, who grinned as Caroline came into the room, and Jarrod Thorne, someone else was present now. A woman of undeterminable age, who coughed incessantly and shivered in her tattered cambric gown, hugged her arms around her emaciated body.

Jarrod Thorne was stirring some elixir which he presently poured into a bottle and handed to the woman. Then he looked at his helper.

'Mrs Anders, this poor creature declares she has not eaten for two days. See that she is given a dish of broth before she leaves, if you please.'

'Oh indeed I will,' the woman answered. 'Come, my dear. Come with me.'

She gave Caroline a little curtsey and before she left she looked at Dr Thorne who added, 'And send Jonathan to me. I cannot imagine what he is about.'

'He was lancing a boil the last time I saw him.'

She gave him one last look which indicated quite clearly her adoration before leaving the room. When she had gone Caroline asked, 'What did you give that woman?'

'Oil of eucalyptus,' he answered without looking at her. 'It will bring only temporary relief, however. She is far gone with consumption.'

'She needs warm clothing,' Caroline said plaintively.

'It is beyond my means to supply clothing, or indeed habitable dwellings which would effect a great improvement.'

The door opened yet again to admit a young man. He was tall and exceptionally thin with a mournful face which could not reassure the sick who came to this place.

'This, Lady Kilgarron, is my assistant, Jonathan Starling.' The young man bowed and displayed not the least curiosity about her and he immediately transferred his attention to Dr Thorne who went on, 'Jonathan, there are two children out there covered with sores. However before any salve can be applied the dirt will have to be washed off. Will you attend to it?'

He had been looking at Jarrod Thorne in a fearful way. Then he nodded, and after giving Caroline a bow as an afterthought, hurried away to carry out the instructions.

Jarrod then went up to the table where the man was still lying, 'How are you feeling, Sam?'

The answer was an incoherent muttering and Caroline was aware that Beth, at her side, was making little sounds of annoyance, possibly because her mistress was not being treated with the great respect and attention she warranted. Caroline was slightly irritated by the lack of it too, although she did understand how busy everyone connected with the dispensary must be.

At that moment Jarrod Thorne turned to give her his full attention at last. He smiled slightly with no mirth. 'Well, Lady Kilgarron, do you find your visit to the dispensary a diverting experience? Does it compare well with visits to Newgate and Bedlam? Or are they the more diverting?'

Caroline felt like striking him. Instead she answered in a level voice, 'I could not say Dr Thorne, as I have never visited either establishment, but I am very much impressed by yours. In fact,' she added, 'I am sure you are short of helpers and I would like to help you here when I can.'

'This is no work for a lady of your standing, Lady Kilgarron,' he answered, not troubling to hide his mockery of her.

Caroline's eyes flashed with fire as her chin came up proudly. 'What would you know about ladies of my standing, Dr Thorne?' He looked startled by her ferocity as she added in a less heated tone, 'If you are scornful of my nursing ability, then allow me to help you in a typically ladylike way.'

To his astonishment she unclipped the diamond bracelet from her wrist and dropped it onto the table. 'The sale of that should realise enough money to provide woollen shawls for poor creatures like the one who left just now. Good day to you, Dr Thorne.'

With Beth at her heels she swept out of the room, through the waiting crowds and back into the street. Her breast was heaving with indignation and not a little from the rash act Jarrod Thorne's scathing words had induced her to perform.

As the carriage set off, she was aware of Beth's incredulous stare. Caroline herself wondered if she had taken leave of her senses. Then she had a vision of Sir Edgar, his face suffused with purple anger at her charitable act of giving away a part of the Kilgarron diamonds, and she began to laugh.

CHAPTER SEVEN

The more Caroline thought about it, the gladder she was she had succumbed to the quixotic urge. That evening as she fingered the magnificent necklace which made up a part of the set, she visualised dreamily how much good the sale of it could do. In fact, she could not contemplate going so far, at least not at that time, but it was something she would bear in mind for the future. As it was, the euphoria remained with her for several days.

She continued to ride early every morning, usually without Polly's company, for their busy evenings ensured her sister slept late in bed.

One morning, several days after her visit to the dispensary, Caroline returned to the house and had only just changed out of her riding habit when one of the maids announced that Dr Thorne had called and urgently requested an audience.

Caroline was both surprised and mystified. Still mindful of his scorn, she did contemplate refusing to see him, but curiosity ensured that she did not, in the end, do so.

After keeping him waiting for several minutes she swept down the stairs, pausing to check that every hair was in its appointed place. Her gown was a fine one of figured silk, pale blue and appliqued with cream lace. It had a low decollete covered by a gauze fischu which nevertheless revealed some white skin heightened by carefully placed patches.

Caroline had never had cause to think about her looks until the people with whom they now associated made her do so. Since then she had become aware that her appearance was a very pleasing one, and that morning she was sure she was looking her best. Why she should be so concerned about her appearance at that particular moment Caroline did not pause to consider.

The footman opened the door to the drawing room into which she had instructed Dr Thorne to be shown. He was standing by the window looking out into the blossoming garden, his hands clasped behind his back. When she came into the room he immediately turned to look at her, giving her that disturbing stare which she could never meet but more than ever Caroline was glad she had taken pains with her appearance and unconsciously began to toy with a curl which lay over her shoulder.

'Dr Thorne you are an early caller. I fancy my sister should be present, but she is not out of her bed yet.'

'I did not call to see Miss Winton. I wished to see you.'

Caroline smiled and came further into the room. 'In that case be pleased to sit down. Perhaps you would like to join us for breakfast.'

'No, I thank you. I have already broken my fast and in any event I shall not stay long.'

His expression remained a searching one and more than ever discomforting. Caroline could not remain still in the face of it and laughed in a slightly nervous manner.

'Then perhaps you will forgive me if I sit down.'

She sank down on the edge of the sofa and he moved then, coming towards her.

'I am somehow of the opinion,' she said, 'that this is not in the normal way of a social call.'

As she waited expectantly for a reply he drew her bracelet out of his pocket and threw it down on a table in front of her.

'Lady Kilgarron, just what did you hope to achieve by that useless gesture?'

Caroline stared first at the bracelet and then transferred her bewildered took to him. His eyes flashed with a fury she could not mistake.

'I . . . fail to understand your meaning, Dr Thorne. I assure you it was not a hollow gesture. You are welcome to the bracelet, I assure you.'

'Thank you, Lady Kilgarron,' he answered with heavy irony, 'but you will have to forgive me for declining your most generous offer. Imitation jewellery may adorn you prettily, but it buys precious few commodities to comfort the poor.'

She could not draw her horrified gaze away from his which did not waver.

'Dr Thorne have you taken leave of your senses?'

'Have you, Lady Kilgarron?' he countered.

'There are those who might well think so. That bracelet is a part of the Kilgarron diamonds and, as such, worth a small fortune.'

'I have had them appraised by two jewellers of repute and I assure you there is no doubt.'

He began to walk towards the door. Caroline watched him go, feeling totally stunned by his revelation. The bracelet winked and glittered in the sunlight, mocking her, and she swept it to the floor with one move of her hand.

As he reached the door she jumped to her feet. 'I vow I had no notion it was not the genuine bracelet!'

He paused to glance at her again and as he did so she swayed unsteadily on her feet. His look of scorn turned to one of concern and he rushed back towards her.

'Lady Kilgarron, there is no need for such distress.'

He caught hold of her and eased her back into a chair.

'Please go,' she gasped. 'I am perfectly all right. Your concern is quite misplaced.'

'I do beg your pardon, Lady Kilgarron. I fear I have behaved in an exceedingly clumsy manner. I should not have come here and told you in such a way.'

'Your anger is understandable, but I do implore you to believe I was not aware of it.'

He smiled then. 'Be assured that I do. Is there anything I can do for you?'

'Yes,' she answered, sitting up straight and belatedly collecting her thoughts. Her humiliation was total. 'You can leave me alone.' She looked up at him. 'If you please, Dr Thorne. There must be many people in need of your services.'

Her tone was such a cutting one he stepped back. 'I am reluctant to leave you whilst you are so distressed.'

'Be assured it was only a momentary shock from which I am quite recovered. I can only regret the inconvenience to yourself. You may be certain I am as much disappointed by it as you.'

'Then will you permit me to summon your maid?'

'I require nothing and no one, Dr Thorne,' she said in a quiet, yet resolute voice, causing him to withdraw further.

'Your servant, ma'am.' He made a slight bow and she let out a long breath as he went towards the door.

'You will not lose by this, Dr Thorne,' she said suddenly. 'I vow I will make reparation for the inconvenience you have been caused.'

He cast her a faint smile before leaving her at last, but Caroline continued to stare at the

101

closed door for some time afterwards before turning once again to take the bracelet in her hand. She crushed it in her fist as convulsive sobs racked her body. After a few minutes of trying to control herself she jumped to her feet and rushed from the room.

As she fled through the hall making no effort to appear composed, Caroline called for her carriage to be brought around, causing the servants to scurry about in alarm. A few minutes later she came down the stairs again, wearing a pelisse and feathered bonnet to see the carriage pulling up outside the door. The footman opened the door and without scarce a pause Caroline hurried out, accompanied by her rather bewildered maid who was carrying her mistress's jewel box.

When they got into the carriage Caroline gave the order to drive to a well-known firm of jewellers situated in The Strand. The short journey was fraught with frustration as the roads were already choked with traffic. However, once she arrived she remained in the shop for no more than ten minutes. When she came out again, the jewel box clutched to her, her cheeks were ashen and her eyes bleak.

Even with a servant to help her she almost stumbled into the carriage and was unable to recall any of the journey back to Queen Square. The first thing she became aware of was Polly, looking concerned as her sister walked into the hall.

'Caro, dearest, I have been so concerned for you. Where have you been? Out on two occasions already this morning.'

Caroline could only stare at her sister, who frowned and said, 'Why have you got your jewel box there, Caro?'

It was then that Caroline looked at it, and it was as if she had never seen it before. Aware that Polly was still looking at her strangely Caroline managed to give her a reassuring smile.

'I merely took it along to the jewellers to have everything checked,' adding hastily, 'I suspected one or two of the clasps were faulty and did not wish to risk the chance of a loss.'

Polly still looked concerned. 'Are you quite all right, Caro? You seem to be less than your usual immaculate self. Your bonnet is an old one.'

'Oh, that is all Beth's fault. I shall have to scold her. It would never do to be seen abroad wearing an old bonnet!'

Polly smiled then, obviously reassured by her sister's manner. Caroline gave the jewel box to the footman on duty in the hall, adding her hat and pelisse before putting her arm around her sister's shoulders.

'Come dearest, let us have breakfast now. I am ravenous after my ride in the Park. It really is most exhilarating!'

*　　*　　*

What concerned Caroline most of all was a fear that Jarrod Thorne would spread abroad the story of her bracelet being a fake. If anyone else were involved she would have been certain of it. An *on-dit* of such a sensational nature was a rare treat and one not to be missed on any account by the *beaux* and ladies of the *ton*.

However, Caroline was forced to admit Jarrod Thorne was not in the ordinary way of *beaux*. He did not paint or patch his face, nor did he dress in the most extravagant manner. True, it was beyond his means to become a dandy, but Caroline was certain he would not have wished to do so in any event. Some would scorn him for it, but Caroline only admired his strength of mind. It must have been very tempting to amass a fortune from people constantly afraid for their health and able to pay any amount for reassurance. That he did not was only to his credit and Caroline regretted more than ever her inability to give her help.

She arrived at the next function on the social calendar feeling particularly hesitant, to discover that not only was Jarrod Thorne not present, but everyone was behaving towards her in the most natural manner. A few days and several functions passed without Caroline catching sight of him, which was both a relief and a disappointment, but she was beginning to breathe easier again. She would be further in his debt and although she had racked her brains continually since his call at the house, Caroline was still at a loss to know how she could make up for the bracelet. It was totally beyond her means to provide the cash equivalent, and the matter appeared to be insoluble until one morning Polly drew Caroline's attention to a paragraph in the *Times*.

'Oh, only listen to this, Caro. There have been riots in Cheapside.'

Caroline had been perusing her copy of *The Ladies' Magazine* but now she looked up sharply. 'I heard some mention of it last night, and find it exceeding odd that riots take place here in London.'

'It appears that it was only one of a number which have occurred of late.'

'For what reason I wonder? Not enclosures surely.'

'Some are of an anti-papist nature,' she read, not without a little difficulty, 'but this was protesting against the high price of food at present prevailing. The military has had to be brought out. It says here that more than a hundred people were injured on Ludgate Hill alone.'

' 'Tis not so far removed from where we are,' Caroline pointed out, 'so I doubt if we may rest easy, although I do have the utmost confidence in the military.' She frowned for a moment or two before asking, 'Would these riots be somewhere in the area of Cannon Lane?'

'Yes, I dare say it would be,' Polly answered absently, frowning with concentration at the newspaper once more.

Caroline suddenly jumped to her feet, ringing for a servant which caused her sister to look up sharply. 'The dispensary will be inundated with the injured,' Caroline told her.

'Not necessarily. There are hospitals in the area.'

'Most people prefer the dispensary and I, for one, cannot blame them.'

'Oh, Caro, you do not intend to go there and offer your help.'

'Certainly not.' The footman came and Caroline said, 'Tompkins, will you ask Mrs Brisley to take out every freshly laundered sheet she can spare, then cut half of them into strips and pack the whole in a parcel? When that is done have the carriage brought round.'

The man's face betrayed no surprise but he did find it necessary to repeat her instructions. 'Half have to be cut into strips, ma'am?'

'That is precisely what I said. Have it done as soon as possible. It is a matter of urgency.'

Polly had been watching her sister in astonishment and as soon as the footman had gone exclaimed, 'Caro, is your attic to let?'

'In all probability, but I do fancy the dispensary will be very short of sheets and bandages.'

Polly grinned. 'I would never have thought of it, dearest, but,' she added with uncertainty, 'I do hope you do not intend to deliver them yourself.'

Caroline took a deep breath. She could not deny she longed to do just that, but after that last rebuff pride forebore her to do so. When the footman returned sometime later to tell her the task was completed she entrusted him with the work of delivering the parcel after all.

It was not until the night of the Duchess of Darnley's music evening some time later that Caroline caught sight of Jarrod Thorne again, talking to Polly of all people. Caroline's heart began to beat loudly at the unexpectedness of his appearance after a considerable absence from the social scene. Her nervousness was to blame, she told herself sternly. He could still denounce her jewels, for she could not be certain of his discretion.

When the entertainment began Polly came to sit by her sister. As Lady Farrowdale's daughter prepared to play the harpsichord, Caroline leaned towards Polly, saying behind her fan, 'You seemed to be in an earnest kind of conversation with Dr Thorne, my dear.'

'He was merely telling me that after the riot victims had been attended to he was summoned to the country for a few days to visit a gentleman who needed his services for an ague.'

Caroline drew an almost indiscernible sigh of relief and settled back to enjoy the music at last. During the interval, before the Italian tenor was due to sing, Mr Underwood came to escort Polly to supper. From the brief exchange Caroline had with him it was beginning to appear that the end result was inevitable now and she was resigned to it. A brilliant match for Polly had never really been more than a wild dream, and her ultimate happiness was all which concerned Caroline anyway.

As she watched Polly go in the company of the man she loved she could not help but smile with satisfaction at what she had achieved by coming to London. She was still smiling when she turned to come face to face with Jarrod Thorne.

Caroline hardly knew what to say. She had found conversing with him difficult enough in the past but since their last meeting it must surely be impossible.

With such thoughts in her head she would have gone past him quickly but then she hesitated as he said, 'Lady Kilgarron, it was kind of you to send the sheets and bandages to the dispensary.'

With some difficulty she forced a smile to her face. 'I only hope they were of use to you.'

'They were indispensable. You must know how many of the injured we took in, in addition to those sick in the ordinary way.'

'It is gratifying to know they were of use. You must have had a dreadful time,' she added.

His countenance fell. 'The dispensary looked like a battlefield for a while.'

A silence ensued and Caroline bridged it by saying breathlessly, 'I must thank you, Dr Thorne, for being discreet about our last meeting.'

'You really have no need to express gratitude, Lady Kilgarron. I should never knowingly cause you embarrassment, you may be sure.'

She smiled, albeit faintly again. 'Nevertheless, I am obliged, more for my sister's sake than my own.'

She was about to move away when she thought better of it yet again. 'Tell me, Dr Thorne, how goes it with the man who broke his leg?'

He smiled. 'It is mending, Lady Kilgarron, although the healing is a lengthy business.'

'It is a great relief to hear it.'

His smile was now a wry one. 'Did you doubt his recovery?'

She began to fan herself furiously, irritated again by his assurance and mockery. ' 'Tis enough that you did not.'

As she turned away yet again he said, much to her surprise. 'May I have the honour of escorting you in to supper, Lady Kilgarron?'

Her eyes narrowed slightly as she gazed

back at him curiously. 'It is kind of you to ask, but Lord Rothsey has already engaged to take me in.'

His smile immediately faded and a look of coldness came into his eyes. Caroline could not help but be affected by it although she did not understand why. Nevertheless, she looked over his shoulder, saying brightly, 'Ah, here he comes now. I have enjoyed talking to you, Dr Thorne.'

Lord Rothsey was a man whose company Caroline had always enjoyed. Young and wealthy, he made no secret of his admiration for her, and yet on this one occasion she wished she had been free to accept Jarrod Thorne's offer.

CHAPTER EIGHT

Invitations continued to arrive at Queen Square every day and Caroline was glad to note that their social obligations filled her diary right up to the end of the Season. Beyond that she dare not look.

'Have you anything there of interest, Caro?' Polly asked as she sipped at her coffee one morning.

'Several routs and various assemblies have been planned,' Caroline replied perusing a clutch of invitations. 'No doubt you know about most of them already.'

'And the one in your hand?'

Caroline glanced at it almost absently. 'Oh, that is only a current statement of our financial affairs from the bank. It is nothing which needs concern you, dear.'

'I'm persuaded we must have spent a prodigious amount of money over the past few months.'

Her sister helped herself to bread and butter. 'It has been worth it, has it not?'

Polly smiled bashfully before saying, 'Mrs Underwood asked me to remind you we are to attend Lady Farrowdale's breakfast tomorrow.'

'I had not forgotten. No doubt Mr Underwood will also be attending.'

'No doubt,' Polly answered wryly.

Caroline looked at her sister then, noting at last that Polly had changed in a subtle way over the past few months. No longer was she so retiring. She was much more certain of herself and whatever the reason for the change Caroline could not be sorry for it.

'You have not changed your mind about him?' Caroline ventured.

'No,' Polly answered, slightly breathlessly. 'I hope you do not mind.'

'I mind only that you are happy, dearest.'

'Your happiness concerns me too,' Polly burst out a moment later.

Caroline looked at her in surprise. 'I am perfectly happy.'

'I do not doubt it, but I do wish . . . Caro, I have never admired you more. The way you have conducted yourself of late has been quite wonderful, and there have been times when I have had to remind myself that you are my sister, but if only you would take your suitors a little more seriously. One of them at least,' she amended. 'This Season could be a golden opportunity for you too. Only see the gifts which arrive for you every day, and yet you display not a partiality for any of the senders. Is there no one you would wish even to consider?'

'It is their motives I suspect,' Caroline answered after a moment's thought.

'They adore you! And not just the rakes

who try to seduce you. Several are quite patently in earnest, Caro, and you cannot wish for more than an offer of marriage.'

Caroline filled her cup with more coffee although in truth she had little fancy for it. 'Ah, but I suspect their reasons are in some way connected with my refusal to take any one of them seriously. It has become a matter of honour, I fear; a good deal of money is at stake by way of wagers, Polly, and I have no wish to be the prize in a lottery.'

The girl looked scornful. 'Tush, Caro! No man would marry merely to win a wager.'

'I am quite certain some gentlemen would do a good deal more.'

'You do know you are being called the Black Widow because you refuse to take a lover or even to consider offers of marriage?'

Caroline remained undismayed. 'I have heard some such nonsense. Our acquaintances are fond of such names, I recall, but in truth they mean nothing.'

'It is also generally held,' Polly insisted, 'that the real reason is because you still retain a hopeless passion for your dead husband.'

'It is a romantic notion and one which will find favour amongst the dowagers, I don't doubt.'

'It is obvious you will not even talk about it.'

Caroline gave her sister a fond look. 'Dearest, there really is nothing to discuss. Be assured I have truly had a famous time since we came to London. There is enjoyment to be had out of creating such myths and mystery, you know.'

As Polly gave her an exasperated look, Caroline went on, 'Enough of such talk, my dear. What are the latest *on-dits* from the tattle-boxes?'

'Most of them are about us.'

Caroline affected a yawn. 'Pray spare me the details!'

'Fanny Thorne has had six offers of marriage and cannot make up her mind which of them to accept.'

'That is of no account, Polly. Lady Farrowdale will make up Fanny's mind for her before long.'

Polly laughed. 'That is very true, Caro. Oh, I did hear of one marvellous story which I must tell you—another about us, naturally!'

Caroline looked at her in some alarm and Polly went on laughingly, 'There is a tale which says we are not all we seem!' Caroline continued to look at her. 'We are said to be two of the King's by-blows, if you please.'

'How ludicrous! ' her sister exclaimed, wide-eyed. 'The King has always been so abstemious and not in the least a rake. I wonder who began such a rumour?'

'Possibly one of your admirers, when in his cups,' Polly answered, her mouth full of bread and butter. 'We have been the objects of speculation since we arrived.'

'There could be worse stories, I imagine,' Caroline mused which made Polly laugh all the more.

'By the by,' she went on a moment later, 'I shall have to instruct the servants to wake me early tomorrow if we are to be at Lady Farrowdale's in time for breakfast.'

'Oh, we shall not go until the afternoon.'

Polly looked at her questioningly and Caroline went on to explain, 'Breakfasts are in the afternoon when they are social events. Few enough people rise before noon, so they must needs be at a later hour.'

Polly groaned wearily. 'I am only just growing accustomed to the late hour the fashionables take dinner.'

A footman knocked on the door and as he came into the dining room Caroline transferred her attention to him. 'A Mr Underwood begs a few minutes of your time, ma'am.'

Caroline looked to her sister who grew immediately pale. 'Polly, are you expecting a call from him?'

The girl shook her head and the footman added, 'He begs to speak with *you*, Lady Kilgarron.'

Caroline pushed her chair back, throwing her napkin on the table. 'Show him into the sitting room,' she told the lackey as she paused to collect her thoughts.

'Caro!' Polly gasped, clapping one hand to

her mouth.

'This hardly comes as a surprise to either of us,' her sister pointed out as she smoothed back her hair before hurrying from the room.

Thomas Underwood was standing in front of the firescreen, his hands clasped behind his back when Caroline entered the room. He looked just then as frightened as Polly, his cheeks pale and his eyes wide with apprehension. Caroline warmed to him immediately.

'Good morning to you, Mr Underwood,' she greeted him. 'Won't you sit down and tell me why you are here?'

As Caroline herself was seated he sank down into a chair too, but looked anything but relaxed.

'It is kind of you to receive me,' he stammered, 'but I knew I needs must come early if I was to find you at home.'

'I am persuaded Polly must have told you I invariably rise at an unfashionable hour, so it is no inconvenience.'

He blushed, saying, 'You are too kind.' She gave him a questioning look and he went on, his cheeks growing redder, 'You must be aware, Lady Kilgarron, that I have been seeing a great deal of Miss Winton since her debut . . .'

'I believe that has been commented upon,' she answered in some amusement.

'Then it might not come as a surprise to you

116

when I ask your per . . . mission to marry her. I am devoted to her, utterly devoted. You need not have to worry, Lady Kilgarron; unworthy as I am, I shall strive to make her happy.'

'From what my sister tells me, you have already gone a long way in doing so.'

He swallowed. 'Oh, that is indeed gratifying.'

'However, one cannot live on affection, great as it might be, Mr Underwood.'

'Indeed. My living at present is not a lucrative one, but in a year or two my uncle—Devonshire, you know—has promised I shall have a better one when the present incumbent retires.'

'That is a great relief, Mr Underwood,' Caroline told him and he became immediately more cheerful.

Caroline felt a hundred years old, having such a proposition put to her on Polly's behalf, but as she had always cared for her sister since their mother died—when the younger girl was born—it was something to which she was accustomed.

When she got to her feet he did so too, looking at her hopefully. 'It is an awesome responsibility which rests upon me,' she told him gravely. 'My sister's happiness is at stake.'

As she walked across the room he said, 'That will be my only consideration as long as I live, aware of how unworthy a creature I am.'

'Oh Mr Underwood, you do yourself an

injustice,' Caroline told him as she rang the bell pull. 'The ability to make another person happy is a considerable one.'

When the servant came in answer to her summons she said, 'Ask Miss Winton to join us in here.' Then she looked at the young man again. 'Polly should join us when we drink a glass of ratafia in celebration.'

His face was immediately illuminated by a glow of sheer pleasure. Uncharacteristically he bounded across the room and took her hand in his.

'You will not regret this happy decision, ma'am.'

'I am sure I shall not, Mr Underwood.'

The door opened hesitantly and on seeing Polly's anxious face in the opening Caroline laughed and said, 'Come along in, Polly. I was just about to suggest to Mr Underwood that we announce the betrothal in the next edition of *The Gazette*—that is if you are in agreement, naturally.'

The girl stared at her sister as if she could not believe the evidence of her own ears and then, giving her newly-betrothed a smile of pure delight, she ran across the room to clasp Caroline close, squealing with delight all the while.

CHAPTER NINE

'Shall I be allowed to tell everyone?' Polly asked excitedly as she and Caroline arrived at Lady Farrowdale's house the following afternoon.

Caroline smiled at her. 'I can think of no reason why you should not. It is, after all, an accomplished fact now.'

Polly clasped her hands together in delight. 'Only fancy, I am actually betrothed! To a clergyman too. Who would ever have believed it possible a year ago? Not only that but I am betrothed before Fanny Thorne too!'

Caroline cast her an indulgent look before she answered dryly, 'Ah, but Fanny has such a bewildering array of suitors from which to choose. I fancy it must be a vexing problem.'

'She will be furious nevertheless.'

Many carriages were waiting in Manchester Square and Lady Farrowdale's drawing room was already crowded when they entered. The countess herself was in earnest conversation with some of her guests but immediately hurried over to greet them.

'The most diverting news! Underwood has come up to scratch at last.'

'Your information is remarkably accurate, Lady Farrowdale,' Caroline replied and Polly asked, 'How did you know?'

119

Lady Farrowdale smiled and nodded across the room. 'Mrs Underwood has been here for some ten minutes, my dear, and could not wait to impart the news. Moreover Mr Underwood has been in high feather, an instance difficult to ignore.'

Polly gasped when she saw her betrothed and, hastily excusing herself, hurried to join him. Moments later a great deal of fuss was being made of both of them. Polly's eyes were bright with pleasure and Mr Underwood was blushing to the very roots of his wig.

Caroline sighed profoundly; she was almost as happy herself and as she glanced around to see who was present she noted Fanny Thorne, one of the Beauties of the *ton*, was for once not the centre of attention, an instance which caused her to frown. This made Caroline smile even more although she knew Fanny normally to be a sweet-tempered girl and not as empty headed as most.

Suddenly her smile faded when she caught sight of Jarrod Thorne too. He rarely attended afternoon functions, obviously because of his commitment to the dispensary. After hesitating a moment she smiled again, with satisfaction this time. Excusing herself from the crowd she had found herself amongst, she made her way towards him.

He was in conversation with several ladies who looked at her with interest as she approached.

'Have you heard our good news, Dr Thorne?' she asked.

'Yes, indeed. Who has not? I have already congratulated Mr Underwood on his good fortune. All that remains is to wish your sister happy. Mr Underwood is the most fortunate of men.'

Caroline eyed him with amusement. 'I too feel that he is, but they are well-suited, I fancy.'

He looked far from happy, she noted, and did not reply. Irritated by his lack of conversation she went on, 'We do not normally look to see you at afternoon affairs, Dr Thorne.'

He gave her a cool, appraising look and she immediately felt trite and foolish. 'There is a very good reason why I am here today.'

Before she could question him further Lord Farrowdale caught her arm. 'Come, my dear Lady Kilgarron, allow me to offer you some refreshments. I cannot allow my brother to monopolise the most ravishing female in the room.'

Caroline glanced coyly at Jarrod Thorne, fully expecting an answer to that, but to her further irritation he had turned away and was now in conversation with a dowager who had been standing nearby, obviously in the hope of engaging his attention.

Lord Farrowdale held no terrors for her any longer and she answered, laughing at last, 'I believe your daughter to be that, Lord Farrowdale.'

He shook his head as he led the way to the dining room. 'A fetching chit, I'll not deny, Lady Kilgarron, but her mind . . . ah, that is a different matter entirely.'

'You are being unfair.'

'I regret not. There is nothing but windmills in her head.'

'Most men demand no more,' she pointed out.

'That is true, but then,' he added in a low voice, 'those are the ones who have not been fortunate to be acquainted with you.'

On the table was a dazzling array of foodstuffs and countless hands were reaching out to avail themselves of some of it.

'You are, as always, the flatterer,' Caroline answered laughingly.

'Would that it had an effect.'

He reached out for a chicken leg which he proceeded to eat whilst he eyed her speculatively. 'Tell me, Lady Kilgarron, do you still retain a pistol beneath your pillow?'

Caroline hesitated before answering, 'Not at all times, Lord Farrowdale. I carry it in my muff during the day.'

Undismayed the earl went on, 'Are you even in danger of being ravished by day, my dear?'

'It is very like, but I should dislike being robbed by some rogue equally as much.'

'Then it appears I must be resigned to

worshipping you from afar.'

'You do me the greatest honour, Lord Farrowdale.'

He gave her a roguish grin which reminded her somewhat of his younger brother, ' 'tis all that remains to me, my dear, if you will not afford me the greatest honour.'

Caroline laughed delightedly at his wit as he consumed the chicken.

'Farrowdale!' His wife's strident tones caused the earl to start and drop the chicken bones.

Lady Farrowdale came up to him and he said, 'What's the pucker, m'dear? Can I not attempt to seduce a young lady without being interrupted?'

She gasped with irritation. 'Two of Fanny's suitors are set to fight a duel. I do beg of you come and stop it.'

'Ha! Would you have me spoil m'own daughter's fun?'

Nevertheless he went off with his wife and Caroline was relieved. 'There is no lack of excitement,' she said to Lady Bleasedale who was within earshot.

Not far away Caroline was aware of Jarrod Thorne who was heaping food onto the plate of a young creature, and she was finding his attentions not unpleasant.

'The Farrowdales can always be relied upon to provide a novel diversion,' the countess replied, her mouth full of lobster mousse.

'Oh, they cannot be held responsible for those men who wish to duel over Fanny.'

'I was not referring to that, which is almost commonplace. If Lady Farrowdale has her way we shall all leave here today inoculated against the smallpox.'

Caroline frowned. 'I am very much afraid I do not understand what you mean. Inoculated? What is it?'

Lady Bleasedale nodded towards Jarrod Thorne. 'A method of prevention if Lady Farrowdale is to be believed. She had Fanny inoculated three years ago and holds her up as an example to us all.'

'Ah, Dr Thorne did say he had a reason for being here and this must be it, but I had no notion what it might be.'

'It is my opinion that Lady Farrowdale goes too far sometimes in her patronage of that young man.'

'Dr Thorne is a great believer in new methods.'

'The point is that this is not new. The very notion of being given some, granted weakened, dose of the smallpox is quite naturally abhorrent to most of us. There is not one iota of proof that the method is either harmless or effective. What he does to those poor helpless creatures in his dispensary is one thing, but inflicting it upon us is quite another.' She smiled then and her fierce expression softened. 'Excuse me, my dear. Felicity Carlyle is beckoning and I needs must speak with her.'

What Lady Bleasedale had told her made Caroline very thoughtful and even when one of her admirers pressed her into conversation she could not give him her total attention. The crowd in the dining room was becoming thinner, everyone returning to the larger drawing room now. Caroline, curious to see what was happening, encouraged her companion to escort her back there, which he did even though he was not happy to relinquish his monopoly of her attentions.

As soon as she entered the drawing room she sensed a great deal of heated conversation was taking place. Polly came up to her with the now familiar flush of pleasure upon her face.

'Caro, is this not the most diverting occurrence?'

'It is certainly novel,' she answered with a smile, 'but I am not altogether convinced as to the merits of it.'

The girl's countenance fell somewhat. 'Thomas has forbidden me to take part but I consider him unreasonable.'

Caroline looked at her sharply, giving Polly her full attention at last. 'He most certainly is not! I entirely agree with Mr Underwood. You must not even think of it.'

Polly's countenance fell even more. 'Poor Dr Thorne, someone must support him, Caro.'

She took hold of her sister's sleeve and led her to the back of the room where they could speak without being overheard. 'Polly, if you are to become a dutiful wife you must begin to comply with Mr Underwood's wishes now. Do you wish to be shown to be unbiddable at this early date?'

The girl drew a sigh. 'No, I certainly do not. You have a good deal of common sense, Caro. I only pray that it may grow upon me before long.'

Caroline glanced across the room, drawing an almost imperceptible sigh of relief. 'Mr Underwood is looking rather anxiously in our direction, dearest. I believe you should go and set his mind at rest.'

When she had gone Caroline returned her attention to Jarrod Thorne who had been explaining his theory and not for the first time, she suspected. He had about him the air of a man already accepting defeat.

'I have proved it to be effective,' he told them.

'On whom?' someone asked. 'The tatterdemalions of Cannon Lane, perchance?'

This elicited a great deal of amusement from the guests but Jarrod Thorne looked furious at their ridicule.

Lady Farrowdale got up to say, 'Shame on you all. Just look at my own daughter—unmarked after three years. 'Tis well-known smallpox does not come twice.'

'We don't want it once!' cried one wit, which caused more laughter.

'The Empress of Russia believed sufficiently to have it done,' Lady Farrowdale continued, but less hopefully now.

'She is not here to tell us so!'

'Won't one of you show the way?' the countess asked, ignoring the calls and jeers.

Caroline's eyes met those of Jarrod Thorne and for a moment which seemed more like an eternity the entire world was far away. Then, as if in a trance, she moved forward.

'I cannot understand this hesitancy in you all,' she said. 'Dr Thorne would not do any of us harm, for who else could pay his high fees?'

This caused a few ripples of laughter. 'If Lady Farrowdale was willing to risk her daughter's well-being we too should be brave enough to take a chance to be free of this dreadful disease.'

Polly looked horrified and rushed forward. 'Caro, you cannot! You cannot and I shall not let you. You forbade *me*, remember, only a few minutes ago.'

'No dearest, I did not. I merely exhorted you to obey Mr Underwood.' She looked then at Jarrod Thorne who was watching her in amazement. 'Tell me what I must do.'

'It is merely a scratch, Lady Kilgarron, in one arm, nothing more.'

'Then be pleased to do it as soon as you may,' she told him, unfastening the cuff of her sleeve.

Some of the other guests gathered around

to watch. Their interest was definitely aroused, Caroline was gratified to see, and a constant murmuring was going on. Despite her outward certainty she was far from happy.

Jarrod Thorne brought a chair forward and she said, 'I shall not faint, you know.'

He smiled. 'I am quite certain you will not. However, it will enable more people to see if you do sit down.'

She sank down into the chair, aware that as many people wished to see her have an attack of the vapours as those who wanted to see the inoculation take place. In any event it was over in a few seconds after Dr Thorne had brought out a small knife from a clean cloth and dipped it into a bottle containing a cloudy substance.

She experienced little discomfort, merely a scratch and after it was over got immediately to her feet, saying, 'I am obliged to you, Dr Thorne. Pray send me a bill for the fee as soon as you please.'

An exciting buzz of conversation broke out amongst the crowd and very soon it was apparent they had lost all their misgivings about the procedure. Caroline moved away, glad to reach a part of the room where the air was fresher as they clamoured to be inoculated now.

'You were marvellous!' Polly cried, rushing up to her. 'So brave. You didn't even flinch.'

'There was nothing over which one should

make a fuss.'

'If it had come to it, I doubt if *I* would have dared.'

Caroline felt rather dazed by her own bravado. 'I cannot help but feel I have made a dreadful mistake,' she murmured.

'I am very proud of you,' Polly insisted.

Fanny Thorne was nearby and she gave them both a disgusted look. 'Such a bore,' she sighed as she moved away.

When Caroline reached the door, she glanced back. Lady Farrowdale was now occupied trying to organise some kind of order in which the inoculations should be done, and Jarrod Thorne no longer looked vexed.

Suddenly, it seemed he became aware of her and looked up, directly at her. For a moment he stared at her expressionlessly before he smiled, almost the smile of a conspirator.

'Are you truly all right?' Polly asked worriedly.

Caroline transferred her attention to her sister then, giving her a reassuring smile.

'I could not be better, my dear.'

CHAPTER TEN

When no ill effects developed over the next few days no one was more surprised than Caroline. That she was able to continue with her engagements amazed everyone with whom she came into contact and a new myth began to form. Everywhere she went she was aware of the way she was now held in awe.

When she had volunteered for the operation, it had been very much a sudden urge with no thought for martyrdom, only a desire to make some small reparation to Jarrod Thorne. However, the admiration of her peers came as a welcome bonus.

The arrangements went ahead for Polly's wedding and the sisters made several expeditions to warehouses in the Strand to make the necessary purchases to assemble a trousseau. The only cloud on the horizon was a further letter from Paris from Charles Brandon, Sir Edgar's cousin. The letter again begged money and Caroline realised this might very well be the pattern for the future. After a short consideration she finally decided to tear it up, burning the pieces in the grate so that Polly would not see it.

Caroline had only just completed that task and was feeling a few qualms about this latest recklessness when the footman informed her that Dr Thorne had called. Again that ridiculous beating of her heart which refused to obey her wish to be calm.

'I shall receive him,' she answered after a moment, bearing in mind his last call on her.

Jarrod Thorne was not a man to make meaningless social calls.

However, when he was shown in Caroline was standing by the fireplace calmly, which belied her inner feelings.

'Dr Thorne, this is an unexpected pleasure.'

'I wished to call earlier only circumstances did not permit, I regret, Lady Kilgarron.'

'You are a very busy man,' she told him in a jolly tone which sounded totally alien to her own ears.

'Busier than ever, thanks to you, ma'am, which is what prompted this call. I wished to thank you for what you did the other day. It took a deal of courage, I know.'

To Caroline's chagrin her cheeks began to flood with colour. 'Dr Thorne, you know very well it was the least I could do in the circumstances.'

'Be assured, then, you have done a great deal. The demand for inoculation is astounding.' He paused before asking, 'I trust that all has been well with you since then.'

He was looking at her searchingly and she gave him a quick smile before averting her face. 'Perfectly. It is no more than you expected, though, is it not?'

'Oh, I have a great deal of faith in the practice otherwise I would not inflict it upon those for whom I have considerable regard.'

Once again she was forced to avert her gaze and he came towards her. 'You may feel proud, Lady Kilgarron, to have saved your friends and acquaintances from an attack of the pox.

She grinned mischievously then. 'Not to mention filling your purse in the process.'

His answering smile was a wry one. 'Indeed, and that, as you know, is a most important consideration.'

'I could not be more pleased,' she told him truthfully.

'You did say you had suffered no ill effects? No fever, for instance?'

'No, Dr Thorne, nothing. Did you expect me to be on my deathbed with pock marks all over my face?' She turned to face him. 'But seeing you have asked I have had an intermittent throbbing in the wound. I expect that is only natural.'

'May I see it, Lady Kilgarron?'

She unfastened the cuff of her sleeve and held up her arm, almost challengingly. He examined it carefully for a moment or two before saying. 'There is nothing untoward here, Lady Kilgarron. It is almost completely healed.'

'Of course,' she answered, withdrawing her arm. 'I would expect no less from someone of your reputation and ability.'

'Your faith is most gratifying. Would that even more people felt as you do. The scourge might well be eliminated in time.'

As Caroline carefully fastened her cuff she asked, 'Dr Thorne, your enthusiasm is commendable, but do you ever think of anything except your work?'

'About as often as you think of anything other than your pleasures, ma'am.'

His tone was mild but it was nevertheless intended to be a cutting one. Caroline stiffened although she owned she deserved that rejoinder, but before she had any chance to move away from him he caught hold of her arm. She gasped as with his free hand he took hold of her chin, turning her face first this way and then the other in the light.

When he let her go at last Caroline did move away from him. 'Dr Thorne, what are you doing?'

'Satisfying my curiosity, that is all.'

'Indeed; curiosity about what, may I ask?'

'There is not a mark on your countenance, which is what I had previously observed, but even so I'll warrant you have already suffered the pox.'

She turned away from him and he said, 'Lady Kilgarron?'

'No, I have not, but you are very astute, for I did cheat a little. I knew, you see, I was unlikely to catch the pox even if your operation failed.'

His expression was plainly disbelieving. 'Yet you say you have not had the pox.'

She straightened up, looking at him directly in the eye at last. 'As you may know I was brought up in the country. When I was a child I was allowed to help with the cows and as a result some sores formed on my hands. They were similar to those of the pox, I was told. It is a well-known fact that milkmaids and the like who have these sores never, ever get the pox afterwards.'

He stared at her in disbelief. 'Lady Kilgarron, that is the flimsiest connection I have ever heard.'

'Nevertheless, it is a belief commonly held in many country areas. No milkmaid, to my knowledge, ever suffered the pox.'

'That was the greatest good fortune,' he answered, 'nothing more.'

She smiled faintly. 'It gratifies me to learn that there are some things you do not know.'

'There are a great many things I do not know, Lady Kilgarron, much to my despair at times. I am for ever trying to widen my sphere of knowledge for there is so much to learn.'

Her eyes sparkled with mischief once again. 'If you curry my favour, Dr Thorne, I may reveal some more well-tried country remedies.'

To her surprise he began to laugh. 'You are the most remarkable woman, and I am lost in admiration.'

'Thank you, Dr Thorne. I am only pleased you do not despise me for my little deception. I did know, you see, that I was in no danger.'

'I cannot hold with that opinion, ma'am, and in any event,' he added softly, 'I could never despise you.'

Caroline was at a total loss as to what to say in reply. She turned away, both pleased and embarrassed.

'You will be attending the Devonshire's ball, I trust.'

'Oh yes,' she answered breathlessly, turning to him again. 'I am told it will be the event of the Season.'

'Yes, it may yet be that,' he murmured, looking at her in a way which was both strange and puzzling.

'May I bespeak the honour of taking you into supper now, before a score others do so?'

'Yes,' she breathed. 'Yes, indeed,' and they were still gazing at each other when Polly came bursting into the room, full of her own news and chatter.

*   *   *

The approaches to the Duke and Duchess of Devonshire's mansion were crowded with carriages on the evening of their ball. The Duchess of Devonshire was not only one of the most beautiful hostesses of the *ton* but a very influential one too. An invitation to any function given by her was greatly prized, and Caroline knew they had been honoured to receive one. The cream of Society would be present, although now that Polly's future was settled, mixing in such circles was no longer of such prime importance. However, Caroline knew it would be expected of them to do so up until the end of the Season.

The mansion was one of the most imposing in London, filled with rare and precious treasures and appointed with the greatest luxury. The night was lit by the torches of the link boys who accompanied the carriages to their destination. In their own Caroline and Polly awaited their turn to climb down with scarce concealed impatience. Caroline herself had not looked forward to any event with such enthusiasm, and both she and Polly had commissioned new gowns for the occasion.

'Everyone will be there,' Polly cried, putting her head out of the window.

'But only one person of importance to you, my dear.'

Polly sank back into the squabs. 'I wish I could say that of you. It would make my happiness complete.'

Caroline merely smiled and still gazing at her Polly asked, 'Caroline, why do you not wear your diamonds any more?'

Caroline kept on staring out of the window and a few seconds elapsed before she answered in a deceptively light voice, 'Here in London they are unexceptional and I feel it best to be unadorned. In the presence of so much jewellery, it is more noteworthy.'

When Polly spoke again her voice was unusually muted in its tone. 'When you married Sir Edgar, I was but a child.'

'Of course you were,' her sister answered, looking at her curiously.

'In mind as well as body, and there was so little I understood. When you told me you were to marry Sir Edgar Kilgarron I was so overwhelmed by the honour of it I could think of nothing else.' She paused before she went on, not without some difficulty her sister noted. 'I am older now. I realise you could never have been in love with him. He was not the kind of man you would have willingly chosen,' she added, and it was her turn to look away.

Caroline gave her a smile of reassurance. 'It doesn't matter in the least any more, Polly. If I had not married Sir Edgar we should not be here now preparing for your wedding or even enjoying ourselves. We must think of the matter in that way.'

'But now I am in love myself I am very much aware of how wonderful it is. I should hate to marry without love, Caro.'

'I have no intention of ever doing so again.'

'I do worry about you. I would like to see *you* settled too.'

'We have discussed this all before, to no avail.' Polly looked so woebegone that Caroline smiled wryly as the carriage moved forward a few paces. 'My dear, Polly, I have no intention of accepting an offer simply to please *you*.'

At this the girl looked abashed. 'I am sure I would not wish you to do so, but when Thomas and I are married we shall be living in Worcestershire. What will you do then?'

The reminder was something to which she had so far given scant thought, mainly because she hadn't wanted to.

'I doubt if I shall keep on the house in Queen Square. That is one thing I am fairly certain about.'

'I shall be so far away from you,' Polly added in a plaintive voice.

'But not for ever, I trust. We shall see each other often. You must not let such thoughts blight your happiness.'

'If only I could be certain what you will do.'

'Perhaps I shall take a house away from London. Brighthelmstone is a village in Sussex of which I have been hearing much of late. The Prince of Wales has become rather fond of visiting it. Mayhap I shall go to live there with Beth, by the sea. I have never seen the sea, Polly, and I am told the air is very healthful.'

She smiled again at her sister as the carriage pulled up in front of the portico of Devonshire

House. 'You and Thomas could visit me there and I shall, of course, come to visit you.

'But,' she added as she climbed down, 'we must not think about that, Polly, for there are too many diversions to enjoy in the meantime.'

The sound of music and laughter was drifting from the house as they climbed the steps. Polly looked up the lines of liveried footmen waiting to receive the guests, and then she smiled at her sister.

'I worry too much, I know, instead of being grateful for all we have. Some day soon I know a gentleman will come along who will make you fall in love with him, just as I did with Thomas.'

Caroline did not answer, but as her sister went up to the top of the steps she frowned for a few moments before following her into the house.

CHAPTER ELEVEN

After they had climbed the great staircase to be greeted by the Duke and Duchess themselves, both Caroline and Polly were immediately surrounded by admirers who wished to engage them for the various dances. As usual Caroline was rather more in demand than her sister especially now that Polly was officially betrothed.

Polly cast her sister a hopeful look and by way of condescension for her Caroline for once accepted each one of them, rather than go into the card rooms with the dowagers.

The ballroom itself was a seething mass of people, all splendidly attired and bejewelled. As Caroline entered, escorted by her first partner she suddenly realised, much as she had enjoyed it, she would not miss the social scene once this Season was over. It had been a strain, although she had borne it well, and she was thankful the end was in sight.

However, to those who considered themselves most fortunate to partner her none of the thoughts were apparent. She sparkled like the chandeliers and their countless candles, conversed wittily and generally charmed all who came into contact with her.

It was not apparent to others either that she frequently cast her attention to the several entrances to the room. Caroline had danced several sets before she admitted to herself that she was anxiously waiting for Jarrod Thorne's arrival and it came as a surprise some time later when she found herself facing him in one of the sets.

'I thought you had decided not to come after all,' she said teasingly, hating the way her spirits soared at the sight of him.

'Lady Kilgarron, you truly could not imagine I would forgo the opportunity of taking you into supper when I have been endeavouring to do so for weeks.'

Caroline's eyebrows rose slightly. 'I was not aware of any particular endeavour on your part, Dr Thorne.'

'Alas,' he sighed, 'that is true. You have scarce noticed me at all, I regret.'

She dimpled prettily. 'That omission is rectified from now on, you can be sure.'

'Dare I hope you have a set free for me?'

'You may hope, but I have none free,' she answered, experiencing both pleasure and disappointment, 'although you shall certainly take me in to supper.'

'I await that time with impatience,' he told her as he went back to his own partner and Caroline to hers.

His partner was no one with whom Caroline was acquainted, but suddenly she hated the poor, dowdy creature most heartily. It was, she realised immediately, her first experience of jealousy and the feeling caused her spirits to rise even further. Dancing with her various partners was no hardship after that when she could look forward to the supper to come.

It was some time later that she found herself at the edge of the dance floor with no partner, fanning herself furiously. The air was quite stifling but no one seemed to mind that. Both male and females used fans to relieve the heat and in the pause between sets the air was filled with the swishing of them.

'Not dancing, Lady Kilgarron?' asked an ironic voice which caused her to look up in alarm.

Jarrod Thorne was looking at her in some amusement and in her confusion she began to fan herself with even more fury.

'I was engaged to stand up with Lord Bowyer, but as you are no doubt aware he met with a slight accident. I do hope he has recovered now.'

'If gentlemen insist upon wearing such high heeled shoes I am very much afraid they will have to take the consequences of the folly. He twisted his ankle quite badly during the gavotte and it has swelled up like an orange.'

Caroline stifled a giggle behind her fan, saying by way of mitigation. 'Poor man. I am exceedingly sorry for him.'

'I wrapped the ankle in a napkin and put him in his carriage with instructions not to stand or walk on it for at least a sen'night.' He hesitated before adding, 'I am persuaded a visit from you during his enforced stay at home would be an invaluable aid to the recovery of his spirits.'

'Did you recommend that to his lordship?' she asked coyly.

'Lady Kilgarron, I would recommend it to anyone.'

Her breath caught in her throat as she looked into his eyes. Then he looked away, towards the ballroom floor where sets for the country dance was assembling.

'Lord Bowyer's mishap is my good fortune. You are free to stand up with me now.'

She laughed delightedly. 'Dr Thorne, did you deliberately make more of Lord Bowyer's injury in order to appropriate his set?'

'Lady Kilgarron, you are casting a slight upon my integrity!' he answered with mock indignation. 'But yes,' he admitted in a more sober tone, 'I could not bear the thought of his trampling your feet so I warned him of the dire consequences of standing upon his own.'

As if in a dream Caroline allowed him to escort her to the dance floor, her heart beating a loud tattoo. The dance was a particularly lively one during which her feet scarcely seemed to touch the floor. Polly, aware that her sister was having an uncommonly enjoyable time, smiled often when they passed close to each other.

All too soon for Caroline the dance ended

and she looked up at him again, laughing breathlessly. He bowed low before her, saying, 'That was worth the lengthy wait I have had to endure to partner you.'

'You should have been more insistent,' she told him.

He gazed at her in a most disconcerting way. 'I realise now that perhaps I should. At least it is not too late.'

'For what?' she asked, flicking open her fan in a coquettish manner.

He looked around and Caroline suddenly became aware that everyone was now moving towards the room where supper was being served, a great banquet no less, set upon silver dishes and salvers.

'How nice to see you partaking of all the diversions,' Lady Bleasedale remarked, glancing at Jarrod curiously. 'Mourning is very necessary, I own, but it really serves no purpose.'

Caroline gave her a half-hearted smile but her mind was still lingering on that last unanswered question she had put to Jarrod. When she looked at him again he took hold of her arm so the others would go ahead of them. She gave him a curious look before he began to draw her back towards a curtained alcove.

'The supper room is in the other direction,' she told him in some alarm.

'Are you hungry?' he asked, pausing for a moment.

She averted her eyes. 'No, but . . .'

'I cannot be alone with you in the supper room.'

'Alone! Why should we be alone?'

Caroline was suddenly afraid, more afraid than she had been for a long time, and yet she knew she had nothing to fear from him.

'So I can tell you that I too have succumbed to your charm,' he answered.

Her eyes opened wide with alarm, for she was far from certain he was being serious. 'Are you gammoning me?' she asked in a low, urgent voice.

He swung her round to face him, exploring every facet of her face. 'Oh no, I have never been more serious in my life. I want to marry you, Caroline. Is that serious enough for you?'

Stunned she could not answer. He still had hold of her arm and her heart was beating loudly again. 'You must be foxed,' she gasped at last.

He drew her close to him, looking down into her face. From nearby came the sounds of revelry. Many people were drunk, most were noisy, but none of them could have been aware of the couple hidden in the curtained alcove.

'Intoxicated only by your loveliness,' he said in a husky voice.

She tried to struggle free of his hold but his lips came down hard on hers before she could effect an escape. At first she felt only revulsion, much as she had done when Lord

Farrowdale had tried to make love to her all those months ago, but then her struggles ceased and her arms went around him. Far from being repulsed she had never imagined a pleasure so intense as this. His kisses all but devoured her, and as she responded at last with all of her being she felt that even her soul had become his.

At last he drew away, looking down into her eyes. 'I, of all men, have the least to offer you, except the greatest love, but is it enough?'

His words should have been the most glorious she could ever hear, but they acted like a douche of cold water in her face and she stepped back, out of the welcome warmth of his arms.

Her eyes were wide, with both fear and wonder. 'No, Jarrod, no! It just isn't possible.'

He looked bewildered by this sudden change in her manner, understandably so, she thought, and her heart ached unbearably with a sorrow she had hoped never to suffer again.

'So it is true,' he said bitterly. 'You still grieve for a dead man.'

Caroline's hand flew to her lips and tears filled her eyes as he added, looking away, 'I would as lief be in my grave if I could be that man.'

She could bear it no longer and tearing her gaze from him at last she lifted her skirts and fled into the corridor. Blinded by tears, she scarce knew where she was going. It did not matter as long as it was away from this man who had somehow stolen her heart and proved that it was as painful to love as to hate.

'Lady Kilgarron! Caroline! Do not rush away.'

She hesitated before she turned, expecting to see Jarrod pursuing her, but a new shock shook her to the very roots of her being as through tear-filled eyes she looked upon the one face she had thought never to see again.

Beneath her rouge she knew she had paled. 'Mr Brandon!'

Dressed in an elaborate toupee, his face liberally powdered and patched, Charles Brandon looked the epitome of the Parisian dandy in his fine silks and brocade. He made a deep bow.

'Lady Kilgarron, I have been waiting an age to find you on your own.'

Behind him Jarrod was coming out of the alcove and immediately he sensed an odd atmosphere as his expression showed. The walls began to reel around her, the floor became unsteady and the last thing she recalled was Charles Brandon's smiling face before her.

*   *   *

The Duchess of Devonshire was smiling too. 'You poor child,' she crooned. 'With such a crush 'tis no wonder more guests do not succumb to the vapours. How fortunate it is that you were on hand, Dr Thorne.'

The duchess moved away and Caroline looked then to Jarrod who was sitting on the edge of the sofa on which she found herself lying. He put aside the vinaigrette he'd been holding and gently pushed back a lock of hair which had come lose and fallen over her cheek.

'Do you feel better now?' he asked.

'Yes,' she breathed.

Caroline thought she could not bear the loving expression in his voice. It was more painful just then than his indifference ever had been.

She raised her head from the cushions to look around. 'Where . . . is Mr Brandon?'

Jarrod frowned and it was the duchess who came closer to the sofa again. 'The Macaroni? Oh, he was most concerned, my dear, but I do believe he has left now.'

Caroline sank back again, drawing a deep sigh of relief. Just at that moment Polly came rushing into the room, her eyes wide with fright.

'Caro! Oh, dearest, what is amiss?'

Jarrod Thorne got to his feet then and walked away from the sofa. Caroline watched him go, achingly. There was nothing she could say to him. Any brief hope she might have harboured was gone now, for ever.

' 'Tis nothing. A swoon,' Caroline assured

her. 'I am perfectly recovered now.'

Polly sank down by the sofa. 'Oh, I am so relieved. I heard only that you had been taken ill.'

Jarrod came back then. 'Your carriage has already been sent for, Lady Kilgarron. Allow me the honour of escorting you home.'

He looked down at her and his face was now devoid of all expression. That brief, passionate interlude might never have happened. Caroline knew she must cast it from her mind too, but it was going to be a difficult task.

She swung her legs over the side of the sofa and Polly got to her feet too. After a moment or two Caroline found the courage to answer him, but she could no longer look at him for fear that all her love and longing would be plain for all to see.

'I beg you not to trouble, Dr Thorne. Miss Winton will accompany me.'

Polly slipped the ribbon of her fan over her wrist and put her arm around her sister's waist. 'I will look after her, Dr Thorne, you may be sure. If you would be kind enough to inform Mr Underwood where I have gone.'

He bowed stiffly. 'Your servant, ma'am.'

Caroline walked slowly across the room, her mind seething with incomprehensible thoughts. She had planned this Season so well and yet so much had happened which she was unable to control. Now Charles Brandon of all people had come back into their lives.

When she and Polly had reached the door she paused to glance back. Jarrod was still standing where she had left him, his face once more an imponderable mask, and yet again she flinched away from his direct look.

He loved her. The thought should have made her heart soar with delight, and yet it merely cast her into the depths of a misery from which there was no return.

CHAPTER TWELVE

Early on the following morning Caroline was riding in the Park as was her usual practice. As she had scarcely slept all night she had decided she might as well do so in the hope that a ride would clear her mind. Her thoughts were still incoherent and she tried to think objectively about Jarrod, instinct telling her that he was in earnest. Ironically she wished he were more like the other men who pursued her; they were often simply wishing to play a game of love much in the same way as faro and hazard. The fact that he loved her proved to be a torment when it should have been a delight.

But in the forefront of her mind was an even more urgent anxiety. The return of Charles Brandon. He threatened her well-being in a way no one else could do.

Caroline dug her spurs into the flanks of her hired hack, racing it across fields of cows in an attempt to force all unwelcome thoughts from her mind. They would not go away but she wished to be free of them for a little while at least.

There were few enough people in the Park that time of the morning which was how Caroline liked it. At that time of the day she was free to be herself. Mid-afternoon was the usual time for riding, when the paths were thronged with aristocratic carriages and well-bred horses.

As Caroline galloped along with the wind tearing at her hat, she felt exhilarated and more alive than she had in years. She was in love, and loved in return and for a while she could revel in the knowledge. Whatever the future held nothing could change that.

Suddenly she reigned in her mount when she saw a familiar figure riding towards her. The horse shuddered to a stop as Jarrod pulled on the reins of his own mount. Her pause was only a momentary one for she began to ride on, digging in her spurs once more, only he forestalled her by riding in front of her horse and snatching at the reins.

'I will be heard, Caroline.'

She sat back in the saddle, closing her eyes briefly. When she opened them again he had dismounted and was coming towards her.

'Jarrod, we have nothing more to say,' she told him in an anguished tone.

'You may not have anything to say to me, but I certainly have something to say to you.'

He reached out to lift her down. When her feet touched the ground his hands were still around her waist and he looked into her face, sensing something of what she was feeling just at that moment, and his lips quirked into the travesty of a smile.

'You need not be afraid; I shall not kiss you again until you give me leave.'

At this she averted her eyes and he released her so she could walk away a few paces.

'What is it you want to say to me?' she asked in a dull voice.

'I, just want to ask you to marry me in the light of day so you can see I am not in the least foxed.'

Her head jerked up and she stared at him, her eyes wide and suddenly moist. 'I . . . thought we had settled that matter last night.'

'I cannot allow the matter to rest so easily. Oh, I do not care if you are in love with the memory of a dead man. I know I can make you happy. What is more certain you can make me happy, for it is impossible for me to be so without you any longer.'

Caroline bowed her head so he should not see the tears begin to slide down her cheeks.

'I realise there are men of great means who aspire to marry you and that I am not worthy . . .

Her head snapped up again. 'You must not say that! You are more than worthy of the finest lady in the land.'

'Then it must be my way of life you object to.' She shook her head and he went on nevertheless, 'I cannot promise to change it. I am committed now because I know I fill a need. It is not the most promising life to offer you, Caroline . . .'

'Please don't go on. It is no use. I cannot marry you. It is impossible!'

She began to go past him, but he caught her arm and swung her round to face him.

'Is it that man you asked for the moment you came to your senses last night? Is he the one you truly love? Tell me and I vow I shall leave you alone.'

Her face was a picture of horror. 'Yes, yes, Jarrod. It is Charles Brandon who stands between us,' she cried and then, shrugging herself free of him, she began to run, back to where the groom was holding the reins of her horse.

He helped her into the saddle and immediately she galloped away without glancing back at all, hoping he would not pursue her and prolong the agony they must both be feeling.

*   *   *

Far from helping her solve her problems, Caroline's early morning ride had caused her far more anguish and it was becoming more and more apparent there were no answers to her problems.

She arrived back at Queen Square feeling shaken and ill, hardly able to face the day ahead, which she felt would be even more fraught than the previous one.

Immediately on her return she handed her gloves and riding whip to a servant and was just removing her hat when someone said,

'You are still an uncommonly beautiful wench, Caroline.'

She twisted round on her heel to come face to face with Charles Brandon who had been sitting in the hall paring his nails with a dainty knife.

'I thought you would lose no time in coming here.'

'I merely wished to make certain we can talk in privacy. From what I have ascertained since my return from Paris a sen'night ago you have become much in demand socially.'

He put the knife away and got to his feet. 'You have done well for yourself, my dear, you and your sister, although it is no more than I would expect of you. You were always ambitious. I am given to understand Miss Winton is actually betrothed to a scion of a noble family.'

'I am very pleased with Polly's choice,' she told him frostily, ignoring his sarcasm.

'I have no doubt,' he answered with a smile, sauntering towards her in an insolent manner which made her anger rise. 'But who would have believed it possible eighteen months ago when you came to Kilgarron Manor? Of course, you spent so much time schooling yourselves in the way of being a lady, did you not? I own that you have done very well, my dear.'

Caroline stood stiff with indignation as he walked around her. 'What I am wondering,' he

155

mused, 'is which of your wealthy suitors you intend to marry?'

'None of them,' she snapped. He looked surprised and then she added, eyeing the footman warily, 'We had best go into the sitting room.' She glanced at the footman on duty once again. 'Please ensure I am not disturbed whilst Mr Brandon is here.'

'Oh indeed,' Charles Brandon agreed. 'How wise. We shall have a little coze, shall we not? Perchance to ponder on old times.'

Caroline preceded him up the stairs. 'This is a very pleasing house, Caroline, but it needs must cost a pretty penny to maintain.'

'I have taken it for the Season, that is all.' Once the sitting room door was closed she asked in a harsh voice, 'Why have you come, Mr Brandon?'

He had been glancing appreciatively around the room but then he transferred his attention to her again, looking at her in some surprise. 'The answer to that is my concern for you, my dear. When you did not reply to my last letter I feared the worst had happened and you had succumbed to some fatal malady or mishap.'

At this Caroline laughed harshly as she walked across the room. 'Unfortunately for you I am hale and hearty.'

'Oh, my dear, what makes you believe that is unfortunate? I am delighted to find you in such robust health, for if anything had happened to you it would have been to my detriment.'

She looked at him again. 'When we last met at Kilgarron Manor I recall that I gave you some money on the understanding you would go abroad and not trouble me again.'

'That was indeed my intention,' he answered, seating himself on a brocade sofa and crossing his legs, 'but I did not reckon that the continent was such an expensive place in which to live.'

She gave him a disbelieving look and he went on, 'Naturally, if it were at all possible I would like to return. I believe that Italy is particularly beautiful and I have not yet visited it.'

Caroline drew a deep sigh as he brought out his snuff box and took a pinch.

'Would that it were possible for me to help you realise that wish. The truth is that I have nothing more to give you.'

His momentary surprise gave way to a knowing smile. 'You cannot have spent everything. I cannot conceive you have been so extravagant.'

'Extravagance on my part is not to blame, I assure you,' she answered in a bitter voice.

He looked rather less bland now. 'You really are a foolish chit, Caroline, if you seek to gammon me in this way.'

'Edgar was sinking in his debts when he died. You should know about that. You shared his recklessness. Gambling, drink, doxies. Any

157

vice which exists was enjoyed by my late husband,' she added bitterly. 'He must have been in dun territory for years. When I sold the Manor most of the money went to pay his creditors.'

Charles Brandon looked angry. 'What a Banbury Tale! You in high feather here in London!'

'What was left after I had sold everything was used to launch my sister into Society. The entire operation, if it can be called that, was carefully planned. Once she is wed I assure you there will be nothing left.'

Charles Brandon looked shaken but then he rallied. 'If what you say is true—and I am by no means certain that it is—you still have the Kilgarron diamonds.'

Caroline smiled grimly. 'I had planned to sell them to provide for myself after my sister was married.'

He began to smile again. 'Very well, sell some of them now. Not everything, naturally, for I am not a greedy man. I ask only for a small portion to enable me to go to Italy and live in the manner every gentleman should. It is only what Edgar would have wished.' His smile turned into something of a sneer. 'If he failed to record that wish it was only because he did not expect to die so soon.'

Caroline threw back her head and laughed. 'The jewels! Fine looking are they not? I thought you might know about them too.

Edgar sold them, probably years ago. What I wear are nothing more than paste replicas.'

Charles Brandon's face suffused with colour. 'You lie!' he blazed.

Caroline's eyes flashed with fury too. 'You may take them to any jeweller you choose and have them appraised.' He looked stunned once again and then Caroline began to laugh again as he got to his feet. After a moment he looked at her again.

'If what you say is true, how shall you contrive to live?'

She looked at him angrily. 'I do not know but it certainly will not be as a basket scrambler on the backs of others, Mr Brandon!'

'No, by jove, you will marry one of your wealthy suitors, will you not?'

It was her turn to look startled. 'I have no intention of ever marrying. Do you think I would ever wish to put myself in that objectionable situation again? I will never marry without love again, nor can I possibly marry for love,' she added plaintively, a vision of Jarrod suddenly coming to her. 'How could I risk anyone discovering what I really am.'

Charles Brandon came across the room and took her arm in a cruel grip. 'How noble of you,' he spat, 'but such sentiments are expensive, my dear, and neither of us can afford them. Of course you will marry again, and soon. You did it once, a drunken old fool besotted with your beauty and youth. It must be easier the second time, and I know just who wishes to become leg-shackled to you, so do not seek to gammon me.'

'No,' she gasped. 'I will not.'

'Of course you will,' he said smoothly, having recovered his composure, 'otherwise I might find the temptation of speaking to a few well-known tattle-baskets on the origins of a certain person. Think how delighted they would be with a few well-chosen *ons-dits* about Lady Caroline Kilgarron!' She averted her face from his so she would not be forced to see his hideous grin. 'I imagine Mr Underwood's family would be most interested too.'

'You are vile,' she hissed. 'You could not do that to Polly. She has done nothing to harm you.'

'My dear, I am not proud to call you cousin. I would prefer to remain silent on that score alone. However, I am certain I shall not be forced to do any other, for you will soon be married and a wealthy lady.'

'No!' she insisted.

'Oh, come now, there must be one you favour. After Edgar there must be quite an attractive choice.'

Before she could tear herself away from his importuning grasp they both became aware of a commotion going on out in the corridor. Caroline was suddenly assailed by the fear that Polly would come in and see what was going on.

A moment later the door burst open, and it was Jarrod Thorne, not Polly, who rushed in, followed by two footmen.

'My lady, Dr Thorne would not . . .'

As one of the footmen stammered an explanation Jarrod Thorne stared at the picture Caroline and Charles Brandon presented, standing close together.

Then Charles Brandon moved away from her. 'One of your suitors I presume,' he said with a smile. 'Well, you always did possess the ability to make a man's blood grow hot,' he added, giving her a lascivious look.

Anger sparked in the other man's eyes. 'Caroline, who is this insolent popinjay?'

'Sir Edgar's relative, Mr Charles Brandon,' she said, swallowing noisily and then to the footmen, 'It is quite all right. Mr Brandon was just about to leave anyway.'

She put a handkerchief to her lips and swayed slightly. The entire situation was too much like a nightmare. Of all times for Jarrod to arrive this had to be the worst.

The footmen withdrew and Charles Brandon, far from taking Caroline's hint to go, sauntered towards the door, watched all the while by the other man. When he reached it he turned, eyeing Jarrod insolently.

'So you are one of Caroline's importunate suitors.'

'And if I am?' Jarrod asked, not troubling to

hide his antagonism.

'I pity you, for you will never do. 'Tis quite obvious, sir, your pockets are to let, so make the most of your doxy before she weds another, someone more able to provide her with pretty gee-gaws.'

'You impudent coxcomb,' Jarrod thundered, clenching his fists.

Charles Brandon looked nonplussed. 'The fair Caroline has a penchant for wealthy husbands, sir, and seeing them off soon after the nuptials.'

Jarrod's face contorted with fury and before Charles Brandon could step aside he had caught hold of his coat and pinned him to the wall with one hand.

'You lying worm. I'll give you the thrashing of your life if you do not beg Lady Kilgarron's pardon.'

Caroline rushed forward, pulling at Jarrod. 'Oh, let him go, I beg of you! He is not worthy of your indignation.'

Her plea had the desired effect and although Jarrod was obviously still furious he did step back. Charles Brandon had grown pale. He pulled at his waistcoat and then straightened his coat before looking at Caroline. His eyes gleamed with malice.

'Not worthy, eh? You say that *I* am not worthy. By gad, madam, you will live to regret that utterance.'

'*Please*, Mr Brandon,' she begged, wringing

her hands together in anguish, 'you have nothing to gain. Be pleased to go now.'

He moved away from the wall and Jarrod, who still watched him. 'I will go, my lady,' he said with irony, 'but before I do perhaps I should tell this . . . gentleman,' he added, eyeing Jarrod with disdain, 'just who he is championing. A hussy, sir. The daughter of a stableboy who flaunted herself in front of my cousin until he was crazed enough to take her for his wife.'

Caroline looked away in despair as Jarrod moved forward again, causing the other man to finch away.

'Enough of this slander! I'll force your lying tongue down your cowardly throat if you do not be silent.'

'Oh, let him speak!' Caroline cried. 'I am done with pretence.'

Jarrod stared at her in astonishment as she pressed the handkerchief to her lips again. Then Charles Brandon cast her a cold look before he continued.

'Not content with her good fortune in marrying my cousin, she conspired to murder him. Murder him, I say! Why else would she pay me to stay away, I ask you?'

'That is not true!' she cried, sinking down on the sofa and burying her head in one of the cushions.

She could not bear to look at the man she loved, to witness his disgust of her.

'Oh, she escaped punishment for it,' he cried, past all caution now. 'The magistrate fell easily for her honeyed lies, but everyone now shall know of it and she cannot deny how her husband died!'

Caroline's body was racked by convulsive sobs. She expected to hear Jarrod storming out of the room in disgust; instead, when she dared to look up again, he had grabbed Charles Brandon once again, by the collar of his coat this time, and was pushing something into the pocket.

'Listen well, poltroon, for I shall not repeat what I say. Here are sufficient funds to take you to Calais. Be on the first packet boat tomorrow, for if you are still in London you will not live the day through.'

'You would not dare to touch me,' the other man answered, in a high frightened voice as he wiggled uselessly to free himself.

'I would not need to soil my hands,' Jarrod answered with satisfaction. 'There are sufficient people with cause to be grateful to me and no means to repay it. They have few moral scruples and hold life cheap so I would only have to give the word for the deed to be done. Moreover, your remains would never be found; I would see to that so make no mistake, Mr Brandon. Be certain your lips are sealed on the matter in which you have been less than discreet today, for if a word of it reaches my ears I shall find you. Oh, indeed, I shall.'

With no more ado he frogmarched Charles Brandon out of the room down the stairs and out into the street. It was much to the amusement of the servants who, aware that something extraordinary was ensuing, had gathered in the hall.

Minutes later Jarrod came back up the stairs, taking them two at a time. When he went back into the sitting room Caroline was standing by the window, gazing out, her hands clasped in front of her.

She was entirely composed now, pale of face and calm, deceptively so. He hesitated in the doorway for a moment to give her a long, hard look and then he closed it with a decisive snap.

'I doubt if you will be troubled by that creature again.'

When she made no reply he quickly crossed the room and put his arms around her. 'I meant what I said. I love you, Caroline.'

'Did you not listen to what he said?'

'Every word. I am sorry he distressed you.'

At this she laughed brokenly. 'You know now that I am not the woman you think me.'

'I think you are the only woman in the world I could love and you could never be the murdering hussy he would have me believe.'

She broke away from him and went back to the sofa, sinking down onto it wearily.

'Mr Brandon did not lie, Jarrod. My father was Sir Edgar Kilgarron's head stable boy.'

'Do you really think I care that you're not

well-connected? It is the last thing I care about.'

'I did kill him, though.'

'Killed or murdered?' he asked in a quiet voice.

Caroline sighed. 'Heaven knows I wished him dead often enough.'

'Tell me about it and let us be done with it once and for all.'

Still she could not look at him. 'He was a drunkard, a bully and I hated him. There was not a day of our marriage I did not wish him dead.'

'People do not die from wishing it, Caroline. How did it happen? If you tell me perhaps it will no longer be painful, and you need not fear the knowledge any more.'

'The night he died he had been drinking, with Charles Brandon and some other cronies who greased his boots. When he came up to my room it was very late—I'd been asleep for hours. Edgar could hardly stand up straight and I knew I could not bear him near to me any longer. The moment he tried to touch me I pushed him away. He was very much in his cups and he grew angry.' Her voice faltered. 'He hit me, but this time I hit him back. Being so drunk he stumbled and fell, hitting his head against the fender. He must have died immediately, so you see, Charles Brandon was correct. I did kill Sir Edgar Kilgarron. Some would call it murder.'

'The magistrate never thought so and nor do I.'

She looked up at him at last. 'Jarrod . . .'

'I have seen much of the results of the brutality of drunken husbands.'

'I can feel no regret at his demise.'

'Has Polly been aware of all this?'

Her face relaxed into the semblance of a smile as he came to sit near to her. 'No, heavens be praised. She was but a child when I married and she was dazzled to go and live at the Manor, and her thoughts went no further than that, although she is beginning to question my former happiness now—or the lack of it.'

'Caroline, why did you marry him?'

'I really had no choice in the matter. My father had just died and Polly and I were virtually homeless. I was quite desperate and his offer of marriage came as the answer to a prayer. I had never liked Sir Edgar, but the marriage, which he considered a great lark against the County families who had long boycotted the Manor, meant security for both Polly and me. I didn't know what a nightmare it was going to be.'

She took a deep breath. 'In any event it enabled me to secure Polly's future even though I did not become the rich widow I envisaged when Edgar died. Even the jewels, you know, are not real.'

'Is this why you have kept yourself aloof

from marriage offers, the fear of being discovered a fraud?'

'I hoped to survive the Season for Polly's sake, but I could not risk anyone I might marry finding out at a later date. Besides, my experience of marriage did not make me at all anxious to enter into it again.'

'And now?' he asked.

She did not answer and he put his arms around her, drawing her close. 'If anyone were to find out who—what—I really am . . .' she whispered fearfully.

'They won't. But if they do I really could not care. No man fortunate enough to possess your love would care in the least about anything else.'

She raised her eyes to look at him at last. 'And I do love you,' she whispered.

'That is all which matters,' he murmured as he kissed her at last.

'This is madness! You needs must marry a wealthy woman,' she gasped, pulling away from him with a great effort. 'I have nothing now, not even my jewels to sell.'

He smiled at her then. 'I have contrived very well without a wealthy wife until now.'

Caroline clung on to him, responding now wholeheartedly until time no longer had any meaning. At last she sat with her head on his shoulder, their hands entwined. All the words had been spoken and all that remained was a future which spread rosily before them.

Caroline had never known contentment before; it had always seemed an unattainable luxury. Now with his arms around her she felt she might drown in her own happiness.

'One thing I must ask you,' he said at last and she murmured dreamily 'Anything, anything, my love. I no longer have anything to hide.'

'Can you please dispose of that pistol you keep beneath your pillow?'

Caroline had forgotten all about it, but at the reminder she sat up and began to laugh. 'I shall not need it any more!'

'Why did you keep it there in the first instance?'

Momentarily she was thoughtful. 'After Edgar died I vowed no man should ever come to my room uninvited. The answer is as simple as that.'

His arms tightened around her once more. 'Be content you frightened my brother half out of his wits. I believe he has been faithful to Augusta ever since.'

'It will not last,' she answered, laughing again.

'It may, for you have spoiled him for all others.'

She gave him a loving look and then he began to kiss her again, blotting from her mind anything save the wonder of his love.

We hope you have enjoyed this Large Print book. Other Chivers Press or Thorndike Press Large Print books are available at your library or directly from the publishers.

For more information about current and forthcoming titles, please call or write, without obligation, to:

Chivers Press Limited
Windsor Bridge Road
Bath BA2 3AX
England
Tel. (01225) 335336

OR

Thorndike Press
295 Kennedy Memorial Drive
Waterville
Maine 04901
USA

All our Large Print titles are designed for easy reading, and all our books are made to last.